FORGED BY SECRETS

DEADLY ISLES SPECIAL OPS, BOOK 3

AMY MCKINLEY

ARROWSCOPE PRESS, LLC

Forged by Secrets

Copyright © 2021 Amy McKinley

All rights reserved. Without limiting the rights under copyright reserved above, no part of this publication may be reproduced, stored, in or introduced into retrieval system, or transmitted, in any form, or by any means (electronic mechanical, photocopying, recording, or otherwise) without the prior written permission of both the copyright owner and the above publisher of this book.

This book is a work of fiction. Names, characters, places, brands, media, and incidents are either the products of the author's imagination or are used fictitiously. The author acknowledges the trademarked status and trademark owners of various products referenced in this work of fiction, which have been used without permission. The publication/use of these trademarks is not authorized, associated with, or sponsored by the trademark owners.

(p) **ISBN-13**: 978-1-951919-05-4

(e) **ISBN-13**: 978-1-951919-04-7

Publisher: Arrowscope Press, LLC; www.arrowscopepress.com

Editing— Kate Birdsall, Line Editor, Taylor Anhalt, Proofreader, Red Adept Editing

Cover Design—T.E. Black Designs; www.teblackdesigns.com

Author photo provided by—Brookelyn Anhalt of lovely.life.photography; https://www.facebook.com/LovelyLifePhotography-102253596490708

Interior Formatting & Design— Arrowscope Press, LLC; www.arrowscopepress.com

1

———

GABRIELA

Caracas, Venezuela
A little over ten years ago

It was the last day of secondary school, and a sense of freedom led a bunch of us to venture out, including my boyfriend of the last two and a half years, Samuel, rather than congregate at my house around the kitchen table. A warm breeze rolled a crumpled piece of old newspaper like a tumble-weed down the sparsely occupied sidewalks.

I cast a nervous glance at the sky, determining how much time we had until the sun set, which would usher in danger. With the anticipated nighttime malice, people would retreat to the relative safety of their homes. Criminals would exit the holes they'd scurried to during the daylight to emerge in an explosion of raised voices and the occasional pop of automatic gunfire.

We had time. Not a lot but enough that I wasn't in a fully-fledged panic. Dusk had yet to settle, and the remaining rays from the sun assured me we were relatively safe. But the sense of freedom that had buoyed my steps fled as our group's youthful outrage in the face of our war-torn country stirred from a simmer to a boil.

Samuel's large hand held mine, and he tugged me down Caracas's once vibrant and bustling city streets. For over an hour, we'd walked through the town where he and our friends pointed out the alarming number of closed businesses in the desolate, politically oppressed area. Most of the people who passed through were on their way home from the few jobs that remained. To stay on the streets after dark invited violence.

Devastation gripped our lands in the form of starvation, lack of medicine, and the loss of jobs far and wide. Few possessed vehicles. Many walked for miles. Those who drove picked up hitchhikers along the road in the way of ride-sharing, as public transportation had ceased to exist in many areas or was too dangerous to take. My heart broke, and my grip tightened on Samuel's hand. Our privileged lives were very different from the majority of Venezuela's citizens because of who our parents were.

I'd let Samuel and a few of our close friends talk me into walking through the city center rather than abiding by our parents' rules of going only to school and our respective homes. We were able to go to one another's houses but nowhere else. There was too great a risk of being kidnapped, as our families had money in a crisis country.

My friends and I shared the same political views and felt a need for action. I'd tried to talk with *Madre* and *Padre*, but they'd hushed my voice, whispering that it was too dangerous, and that the president wasn't in his right mind. To me, that indicated an even greater need to do something. We wanted to push for change, but I wasn't sure we were doing it the right way.

My bravado from moments earlier withered to a sudden death. Our families orbited within the president's inner social circle, affording us a sense of safety and bounty that the rest of our country was deprived of. Out in the open, witnessing men and women with baggy clothes that had seen better days telegraphed a tangible loss of hope.

My focus snapped back to what was going on around me, to my tall, lanky boyfriend, whose passion for change infused the air with crackling intensity, a vibe that left me oddly frightened and wanting to duck my head and flee.

"What's happening to our cities is criminal." Samuel raised his arm, letting my hand fall from his fingertips as he turned to take in the repressed area. "Our families have the power to influence change, yet we've done nothing. That ends today."

Our friends cheered beside Samuel, all except me. The fine hairs on my arms and nape stood, warning that someone watched with ill intent. My gaze skittered nervously along the sidewalks, from face to face.

Despite the afternoon heat, a shiver of dread crawled over my body. I studied the people at the edges of the town where my boyfriend made the street his stage. We'd pressed what money we'd had on us into people's hands, wishing we had brought more. I searched the handful of hopeless expressions until landing on a menacing presence standing apart from the dull and lifeless ones. He wore clean black pants and a button-down shirt, and his penetrating gaze bore down on me. *No…*

I recognized him from events we'd attended with the rest of the president's close friends and associates. The man in the black clothes with a gun strapped to his waist and a dangerous demeanor worked for the president, and he was… not good. I tugged on Samuel's shirt as the man took a casual stance outside a boarded-up pharmacy. The government had ceased to approve shipments of medicine some time ago.

"We have to go," I pleaded, jerking harder on his shirt.

He lowered his arms, turning to me with questions in his warm brown eyes.

"It's not safe."

Red tinged his cheeks, and his eyes lit with challenge. What he wanted to do was such a bad idea. I agreed with him and our friends that something had to be done to help the people, but we were, in a way, exempt because of our political favor. For us, not much had changed, but for a majority of our country, everything had. Our stomachs didn't cramp with hunger. If we were sick, we had medicine at our fingertips, and we were able to quench our thirst with an abundance of water.

"This is why we came here, Gabi." Maria dropped the fist that she had raised in support of Samuel's outspoken views. She rested her palm on a jutted hip and swept her other hand out in a flourish of self-righteous attitude. "Are you saying we should do nothing? Our parents—yours specifically—have the power to influence change. We need to take action."

Tears threatened, and I tried to hush her, but nothing worked. They were excited and drunk on the idea of being able to make a difference. I understood because I was of the same mind, but that man brought reality crashing over my head. There weren't enough of us, and we stood out as easy targets, especially with one of the president's militia watching our every move.

I stepped around Maria, so I was in front of Samuel. Wrapping my arms tightly around his waist, I tipped my head back until our eyes met. "Please, take me home."

I wanted to tell him it wasn't the right way to do things, that to affect the change we wanted, we should be lost in the masses of people demanding action. To draw attention to us, to our families, was a sure way of stifling our voices by putting pressure on our parents.

There were other ways we could help, and we needed to regroup and explore those options. I also wanted to talk with my parents, as I knew they secretly shared our desire to aid our people. There had to be a reason they weren't doing anything, and I wanted to know what that was and how they thought it would be best to overcome the obstacles that stood in our way.

Tears swam in my eyes. Samuel frowned, concern etched along the lines bracketing his mouth. "Okay, yeah, we can do that." He took my hand in a firm grip and led us to a waiting car.

Maria and a few others argued against leaving, but Samuel calmed them, saying we would regroup and strategize back at my place. My mind was already spinning about how I wanted to formulate a way to get as many people from our school as possible to rally together in protest against the government and how they starved our people. That was something they would get behind and would provide a way that I could join in without going against my parents' wishes that I not draw attention to myself. That rule was a new one, in addition to a coded phrase to indicate trouble, and had been uttered over a rushed breakfast before my parents and I went our separate ways for the day.

My only hope was that the menacing man I recognized didn't do the same with me. The closer we got to my home in the meticulously maintained gated community, the more I was able to push what'd happened from my mind.

It didn't take long for us to return, grab snacks, and continue our spirited conversation about how to save the people as we crowded around the large kitchen island in my home. The tension that had taken residence between my shoulder blades slowly dissipated as the sun began its descent, ushering in evening shadows. But it all returned as the sky darkened further and *mi padre* entered the kitchen in his fashionable dark-gray suit, his tie loosened and off-center, and his face a mask of calm that contrasted his harsh command that everyone needed to go home immediately.

When the door closed behind Samuel and my friends, I twisted the ends of my waist-length hair between nervous fingers, readying myself for the storm that was sure to follow. And it did, just not in the way I'd thought.

Padre ran his fingers through his dark hair, mussing it, while Madre wrung her hands before flinging herself at me. The sound of the faucet then the radio filled the eerie stillness of the house.

Madre held me tightly in her arms, her shoulder-length rose-gold hair mixing with my matching hues as she rested her cheek against mine. The scent of lilies from her perfume cocooned me in familiarity. Her body trembled as she whispered, "I love you more than life, my sweet." She squeezed harder, her soft, melodic voice pinched with despair. "You have to go."

Stunned, I could only return her hug until Padre pulled her back with heartbreaking gentleness. His hug was fierce, and I strained to hear his hushed words. "We love you, Gabriela, and that's why we have to send you to your aunt and uncle in the States, where we know you'll be safe."

"Just for a little while." Madre's voice cracked, and she took a deep breath to compose herself. She cast a glance at my father before pasting an attempt at a reassuring smile on her face. She reached behind her neck and unclasped the gold locket necklace with a turquoise inlay.

Padre took it from her and popped it open, revealing pictures of us and a mini USB flash drive inside. Closing it, he fastened the delicate chain around my neck, and Madre slipped it under my shirt, hidden from view. "Give this to your uncle immediately when you see him," he instructed. "On it, there is documentation about our government and the many injustices done to our people. It's your ticket to safety, a passport for a new life. We'll follow as soon as we can."

I wanted to argue, but their panicked expressions stole my words, and I took my backpack and purse, which Madre pushed into my hands.

"They'll have clothes for you, but this way, you won't look as suspicious as if you didn't have any bags," Padre explained as he handed me my hoodie. Once it was on, he pulled up the hood and tucked my hair inside. "The car is already out back with instructions. Hurry."

We left the kitchen's brightness and traveled through the back of the house, not turning on any of the lights. I peered through the side window by the back door and found my parents' driver waiting with the headlights off and the car engine running.

There was time for one final hug. I memorized the floral scent of Madre's perfume, and Padre's strong embrace enveloped me while we whispered, "I love you." Then I went from the unlit back door, across the yard, and to the idling vehicle. Once inside, tears ran like a river down my face, and I felt like I was going to be sick.

I twisted in my seat as the car sped from the back of the house, rounded a corner, then turned back onto our street but traveling in the opposite direction. I craned my neck, wanting one last glimpse of our home, but we were too far and going too fast.

The vibration of a text buzzed at my hip, and I pulled my phone from my jeans, praying it was my parents ordering me back, that their sending me away was a mistake.

My heart thundered in my ears as I read Samuel's text: *I feel responsible cause you got in trouble. I'll talk to your parents.*

My hands trembled, my fingers hitting the wrong letters as I tried to tell him not to go there. To go home.

Another text came through before I could even send mine: *I'm here.*

A loud boom sounded, and the car shook. My heart stopped. I dropped the phone and scrambled to my knees. A large plume of smoke rose in the distance, right over my house, where my parents and Samuel were. A high-pitched screaming noise rang in my ears. The car swerved to the side. My door was flung open, and the driver grabbed hold of my shoulders, his face frantic. His lips moved, but I couldn't understand what he said.

Then I realized the screaming was coming from me.

My mouth snapped shut, and I swallowed the horror as I realized the magnitude of what we'd done by taking our grievances to the street, the repercussions of our actions in the heat of the moment, and how it would implode to affect those I loved. Madre, Padre, and Samuel were dead, and it was my fault.

The boy I thought I would grow up to marry had been taken from me.

Gut-wrenching sobs shook my body as my heart broke for those I loved. I clutched the locket with the pictures of the three of us inside that Madre had given me and the hidden flash drive that would be my ticket to a different life and a new name —Malina.

2

MALINA

Las Vegas
Present day

My entire body tingled with awareness as Tyler, one of the Navy SEALs I worked with as logistical support, stood by my side. Flying with friends to celebrate our colleague Mark's birthday in Vegas had sounded like fun until my friend Anna told me later that Ty was also coming. We didn't get along. He was hot as hell, but we'd gone out once before. The night hadn't gone well from the start. I mean, he'd arrived at my apartment on a Ducati, and I'd been wearing a dress.

We'd taken my little Honda instead. I would have loved to say things got better after that, but they didn't, at least not at first. The conversation was lacking. We were both preoccupied and seemed to have no interest in getting to know each other. But the chemistry between us was off the freaking charts, and I'd been careful to keep my distance. If we hadn't had to talk to one another, the night would have been perfect. It was Ty, after all, the guy who made me have to check myself for drool whenever he walked by me in our high school's halls. Not much had changed.

On our date, neither of us had been all that hungry, so we sat at the bar. A few drinks in, and those good intentions to keep my distance went up in smoke. We decided to go dancing at a club. One thing led to another, and in the coat closet, I'd climbed him like a tree.

I snorted at the memory—I'd told him he was annoying and to shut up and kiss me. The look of irritation on his face from my outburst morphed into lust in two seconds flat. It was a miracle we weren't caught.

On the way home, he'd insisted on driving my car, which seriously pissed me off. I'd seen him treat other women well, but we were at each other's throats more often than not. We hadn't been friends in high school. When I wasn't drowning in grief, I was a quiet, nerdy mathlete who loved robotics club and chess. He was a popular jock, dating this cheerleader or that gymnast. We did not inhabit the same circles. But I'd known who he was even then and maybe had developed a little crush, which died a swift death that first date.

He was cocky. I was mouthy. Brains meeting brawn meant a collision.

Don't get me wrong—Ty was a SEAL. He was freaking intelligent, just not a self-proclaimed nerd like me.

In all actuality, it was a good thing he drove, as I'd had one too many Long Island iced teas. Drunk with lust, I'd let him reroute us to the marina, a boat, and a short trip to his family's island for an entire night in his arms, where he'd started to call me "Island Girl." It was the stuff dreams were made of, knowing nothing would come of it the morning after. With a past like mine, I couldn't risk what remained of my heart.

I wasn't thrilled with the news that he was coming on the Vegas trip that a friend from work had orchestrated.

I wore my stretchy washed-out blue-gray "nerd-girl" T-shirt, sure to turn him off and keep him at a distance. Our disastrous hookup predated even my last boyfriend, and that had ended badly over a year before.

Avoidance was not an option, as I was support to his SEAL team. The friction between us at work was thick. When his deep-brown eyes followed my every move in the office, I swore he glimpsed my darkest secrets or cataloged my most intimate fantasies, something I had no doubt he could fulfill. But my heart had been promised to another and currently resided alongside Samuel and mis padres, six feet under.

Ty was a save-the-world type, something he'd shown evidence of back in high school when he'd shielded me from wannabe boyfriends by whispering words in their ears that caused the aggressive jerks never to bother me again. He wasn't afraid to fight for what he believed in, a trait that I was innately attracted to, but I couldn't forget where that had gotten Samuel.

It was better that I did what I could to push Ty away, and I had been since that spark of interest that betrayed my love for Samuel back in my first year living in Honolulu. In those days, I'd noticed his interest, but I didn't have anything left to give and had been terrified to draw any attention to myself—which was impossible to maintain anywhere in Ty's orbit. Old habits died hard, and the possibility of a relationship with him sent my body into immediate fight-or-flight response.

I toyed with the necklace around my neck that held pictures of mis padres but was empty of the tiny flash drive Padre had instructed me to give to Dad, aka my uncle Matt. A large part of me had died with them, which made it difficult to let others in. I'd dated, but they were always safe men I knew I wouldn't lose myself to. That was what made Ty so dangerous and why I had a tendency to run from him—he had the power to destroy what remained of my heart.

It didn't matter that my fingers itched to roam over all that rippling, tan Hawaiian skin or that I craved the way his lips and hands played me like a fine-tuned instrument—I couldn't risk what was left of my heart. I did what I could to avoid Ty, especially his touch. Those casual brushes against his well-defined arm while getting coffee at work sent an electric shock followed by heat spiraling through me.

We'd never tried to repeat the explosive interaction we'd had on that one date. I had been in a dry spell for a while and had to admit that I was tempted by him. But he was not boyfriend material.

———

Tyler

Las Vegas

MALINA'S green eyes flashed fire, reflecting the extravagant lights in the Vegas casino. She pursed her pouty lips, clearly annoyed, and I grinned in response. Her long rose-gold hair framed her gorgeous face and fell in loose waves down her back to her small waist. I had to fight from running my fingers through the thick mass then over her tight little body.

She'd made sure not to get too close on the flight over. I'd sat in the back, and she'd taken a spot in the front of the jet. The limo ride after had us positioned across from Mark and Anna, and she did everything she could to maintain distance. I'd flirted with her by changing seats on the jet to sit next to her, brushing my fingers along her arm when I talked, and leaning close to point at something outside the window. She was fuming, her fingers threaded together in a tight grip most likely to keep from shoving me, and I was more than turned on.

She probably thought her nerd-girl T-shirt was a natural repellant for a guy like me. She was wrong. I couldn't be more into it. Smart, sexy women were hot as hell, and Malina drove me out of my mind. I'd stayed away in high school because of her haunted eyes. Grief had clung to her like a second skin, the same cloak that had rested on Kayla Kane's shoulders our senior year in high school. Kayla was my brother's fiancée.

Back then, I had been drawn to Malina's brilliance despite the cloud of sorrow she hid behind. Over time, she'd shed some of the darkness, and her soul-deep beauty shone through her sun-kissed skin. Her personality had the ability to both calm and challenge. Lina was a different person from those days, and I was even more drawn to her as an adult then I was in high school. Quick to laugh and equally so to anger, she kept me on my toes. The small huff she made when she was exasperated by my leaving random stuff on her desk or the skittish way she tried to avoid me only made me try harder.

She'd freaked after our second date, calling our night a mistake even though it was anything but, and I'd given her space because a relationship with her was the stuff my dreams were made of.

The timing had been all wrong, though. For as much as I'd wanted to pursue her, I was set to deploy soon after we got together. For the entire duration of the mission, she never left my mind, and that told me more than I needed to know. And based on the disastrous missions of late where bad intel had caused the loss of lives, time wasn't on my side, which meant that night in Vegas was an opportunity I wouldn't let slip from my grasp.

The woman would be mine. She just didn't know it yet.

3

———

MALINA

Five weeks later

A door slammed in the Pearl Harbor office where I worked under Mark as support to SEAL Team 9. There was always someone coming and going. My fingers flew over the keyboard as I did my best to block the usual office chatter, keeping my head down, determined to finish the report Mark needed before I dove into the rest of my work. My stomach growled loudly, and I shot a sideways glance at Anna, who headed my way. We'd made plans for lunch. I glanced at the clock on my computer and was surprised that so much time had passed.

The volume in the office kicked up a notch. I barely registered the commotion or the deep voices that I knew belonged to a few of the SEALs, but one in particular stood out. I wasn't turning around to see him walk through the door, though.

"Hey," Anna leaned on my desk, her gold bracelets jingling. "Want to try that new sandwich café for lunch?"

"Oh, I've been dreaming about that place." I cast a wary glance at Mark's desk—those two had been all over each other lately, and their lovey vibe was difficult to be around at times. "Is Mark coming?"

Anna's dreamy expression made me sigh with longing to have what she had. I was always such a chicken. "No, Mark isn't coming. He has too much work to get through. I said we would bring him back something."

Ty neared my desk, coffee cup in hand and—I narrowed my eyes—another DVD clutched in his other. Ever since we hooked up, when he was close to going on a mission, he'd drop a movie on my desk and say, "We should watch this when I get back." I suspected it was his version of "Netflix and chill," the universal code words for sex, and even though I had to mentally fight not to launch myself at him, it couldn't happen. Besides, there was always a message in the movie title or story line explicitly meant for me, as if he aimed to prove we weren't a mistake.

I had a drawer full of movies he'd given me, including *How to Lose a Guy in 10 Days*, *It's Complicated*, and *Sweet Home Alabama*. The main theme was how I'd run away. And I had because, well, it was complicated!

And I was cautious—Ty was a man whose deep voice promised a lifetime of love and support. His ready smile and steadfast loyalty to those he considered family or part of his brotherhood was infused with honor and integrity. From his sculpted athletic form, his chiseled features, and head-turning presence, he was too gorgeous, too everything, which included unattainable. He was the one I could lose my heart to, and if something happened, I didn't think I would survive it again.

Anna thought our interactions were sweet. I thought the whole situation was dangerous and hid my vulnerability behind annoyance.

Joe, another SEAL, walked next to Ty and said something to make him laugh. When he looked my way, it was to wink at me with a silent salute of his mug. Then I caught a glimpse of the soon-to-be mine movie, *Runaway Bride*. My irritation with him spiked. And on top of everything, he liked to leave his coffee mugs on my desk, which caused even more interaction. I snapped my focus back to Anna. I had to get out of there.

"Let's go now. It's only a few minutes early, and I'm starving." My fingers curled around my purse strap, and we rounded my desk. I panicked a little at the thought of passing Ty. It would be a tight fit to go around him as he always took up so much room, and only vigilant awareness stopped me from gravitating toward him. Everything about him was sensory overload. He had that effect on me and always had.

As usual, my vision tunneled when I got close to him, and the rest of the world faded in comparison. Anna was talking to me, but I couldn't focus on her words. My pulse kicked up a notch as I zeroed in with wild need on what his lips promised. I caught myself just as my body drifted toward him.

I shouldn't have bothered because as I passed, he shifted his arm slightly, brushing against mine. Tiny electric zaps traveled through my body from the brief touch, and I sucked in my breath. Everything about him hurtled me into a hyper-aware state. The attraction between us made me dizzy with want.

I knew what was coming. He would ask me out and possibly tease or annoy me. Sometimes, I gave it back to him. In a way, our back-and-forth was fun, but going out with him again wasn't a good idea. Samuel, my boyfriend from secondary school, always found a way to come between us. I was constantly reminded of the love we had, the loss, and the potential aftermath if I let myself fall for Ty—what could happen to him. The problem was, I was already halfway there.

"Lina." His deep voice found my ears, and I paused before shaking off the thrall he had over me.

"Ty." My breathless reply sent a shock wave through me but not enough to shake his mesmerizing hold.

With a flick of his wrist, he held up the movie, amber eyes smoldering with desire that underscored the words coming out of his mouth. "I got you something. Thought we could watch it over the weekend or when I get back in town."

The spell was broken. I jerked back a step, severing the heat of his arm at the reminder of how disastrous we had been together, especially given my attraction to him that teetered on the edge of falling in love.

4

———————

TYLER

Venezuela
One week later

A hot, humid breeze stirred the surrounding trees and bushes that I used as camouflage. I was flat on my belly with the target building in sight and sweat trickling beneath my shirt. Rich, Joe, and I silently moved forward then entered the water to infiltrate the El Palito port off the Venezuela coast, the refinery where Iranian tankers docked and unloaded barrels of what they claimed was oil.

After Venezuela ordered an evacuation of American workers then seized the US Embassy employees who didn't comply fast enough, our unit had infiltrated and freed the majority of the hostages, but five remained. A small unit of SEALs stayed behind to secure those in captivity. We'd located them by satellite then tracked their transfer to the refinery.

We'd been watching the shifts for an hour. The harbor building was well guarded, but there was a gap when the guard turned the corner. They had additional patrols on the roof, but we could circumvent their field of vision with a water approach.

Under the harbor's dock, I moved silently through the water, careful not to make a sound. We traveled in a single line, Joe and Rich at my back. Hidden beneath the planks and by dark of night, we advanced on the target, the harbor building where the Iranian tanker had unloaded what they said was oil to help a friend, the war-torn, poverty-stricken, and starving nation of Venezuela. The Iranian president was chummy with Venezuela's ruling governing body.

The Navy knew it was bullshit. Everyone did, but the threat from both parties was to declare war if our Navy's ship and sailors moved in to inspect the contraband. We had good intelligence suggesting that weapons were inside those hundred or so barrels stored in the very building we stalked. It was no secret that both rulers despised the US.

With Americans detained, our covert mission was to go in, recover the hostages, and report on any weapons found. The three of us had orders to retrieve the hostages and get film on the weapons.

Beneath the harbor dock on the waterfront side of the building, we paused as gentle waves lapped beneath our chins. The acrid odor of smoke drifted down as the guard exhaled then crushed the cigarette beneath his booted foot. As his footsteps continued toward the side of the building where he would turn, Joe squeezed my shoulder. My fingers curled around the edge of the dock. I heaved myself from the water, holding still to assess the risk of discovery.

No alarms were raised from the roof guard. Keeping to the shadows, I crept forward as Joe and Rich followed. We hugged the side of building. There was less than one minute before the next guard would round the corner.

The guard we watched continued to walk the perimeter, about to turn the corner. Rich eased from the shadows, took him out, then lowered his body into the shadows. We had a few seconds before the other sentry made an appearance.

Machine gun held across his body, the next guard approached. Joe slipped behind him, slitting his throat. Joe yanked the gun away from the dying insurgent then dragged him behind a crate, where he would bleed out in relative silence.

As we maneuvered along the outer perimeter, we donned infrared goggles. Two guards were stationed at the refinery's entrance. I eased around the building. Joe and Rich fell into line behind me. The guards never saw us coming.

With the stationary guards down and dragged out of sight, we entered the building, which was similar to a warehouse. Narrow passages branched off to what we were told would be several small offices. Barrels lined a large portion of the open space, the scent of salt water and oil heavy.

The building was oddly empty except for an occasional noise off to the left. In a single line, we moved on silent feet to the hallway that led to the offices where the hostages were suspected to be. As we inched down the corridor, we cleared the rooms until we came to the first locked, windowless door. Rich retrieved tools from his pocket to pick the lock. We aimed for stealth. Kicking it open wasn't in the plan just yet.

After a handful of seconds, the door swung open, and Joe and I flanked Rich, our guns drawn and ready. The room was small, dark, unguarded, and filled with the hostages we sought.

Rich moved forward, assuring the frightened captives we were there to rescue them while I took point at the door. Joe helped to assess and gather the people. They weren't in good shape. There were four in total, beaten, dehydrated, weak, and barely able to stand. We needed to get them out of there and home quickly. Those who could help wrapped their arms around a fellow captive who needed the support. In hushed words, we explained how we were going to make our exit. In a single line, double if they were helping one another to walk, we would travel down the hallway and out. Rich took the rear, Joe point, and I flanked the side. They would hug the wall.

There was supposed to be five of them. We had to make sure their coworker wasn't already dead and paused before exiting. "Is there anyone else here?" Joe whispered to our group.

A man with a thick white beard caked with dried blood nodded. "Yes. They have Anthony."

An anguished bellow echoed along the corridor, and I exchanged a wary glance with Joe. The naked pain in the cry infused the air around us, and the hostages cringed. The man closest to me whispered that their captives also had his wife, Celia.

With hand signals, I coordinated with Joe and Rich to take the hostages we'd secured to a safe distance outside the building where we'd done our recon.

Intermittent roars of agony followed by gut-wrenching sobs made it easy to locate the last hostage and, hopefully, his wife. But her odds of survival weren't good, based on what I was hearing. I blocked all thoughts except the mission. *Rescue the hostage and get him to safety.*

My 9mm led the way down the hall. My senses were on high alert. The metallic stench of blood permeated the space. The man's sobs quieted, and the deep undertones of someone else speaking carried to the hall but were too quiet to make out the words. No sounds indicated there were others than those two in the room. Wet footprints trailed behind me from our sojourn beneath the pier. Straining my ears to pick up anything else, I edged along the wall, pausing just before the entrance. I had the element of surprise on my side but probably not for long.

With a quick pivot, I entered the room and catalogued the threats within the first second. An insurgent stood behind the hostage, leaning over him and speaking into his ear. With a squeeze of my trigger, he crumpled to the ground. I caught movement to the right and fired two more rounds, chest then head. Another dropped. The room was clear of threats, but those on the roof would be coming in hot.

I did a quick assessment of the hostage. One eye was swollen shut. Blood dripped from a gash on his head, and his lip was split. Tears coated his face, turning some of the blood pink. At his feet lay a partially dressed woman, her dark hair a tangled mess obscuring her face. She lay in a puddle of her own blood.

I bent and pressed two fingers to her carotid. There was no pulse. The man's gaze remained on her, no recognition or sound coming from him. He was in shock, and rightly so. Pulling my knife from its sheath, I cut him loose. "I'm here to take you home."

As I pulled him to his feet, my arm supporting most of his weight, we maneuvered around the dead woman. His head jerked to where she lay, and he struggled in my hold.

"I'm not leaving." While his voice was gravely and broken, there was a core of strength and determination woven in.

My mind warred with my heart. I knew what he was thinking. I understood. If Malina had been threatened, I would have gone to great lengths and inflicted a lot of damage. "My orders are to bring you home."

He regained some strength, standing on his own, and pulled away. "They have to pay. What they did to her—" A sob choked his words.

I urged him to keep moving while he got himself under control.

"I'm not leaving. Not yet. I know where the weapons are. I heard them. And I have more information, but I'm not giving it to you unless you help me."

We needed those coordinates. And I couldn't begrudge the man his revenge, not if I was able to help him and get the Navy the intel they needed to stop a potential war. "It's not safe here. I have to get you out. When we meet up with the rest of our group, we can negotiate." I shouldn't have agreed to anything, but I wanted to put an end to the threat against us too.

Anthony took a second to scrutinize me with his good eye. Whatever he saw in my face answered his question. With a curt nod, he stopped fighting me.

It was eerie how there weren't other soldiers on the premises. But I didn't dwell on it, assuming Rich and Joe had neutralized the remaining two from the roof, and got the hell out of there. Once outside the building, I kept us to the shadows. We wove through the marina, down a hill, to where we had a boat waiting under the cover of a few jutted rocks and shrubbery.

Joe and Rich had the hostages secured on the boat. They stood guard, waiting for us. But we weren't going. I was going to deliver proof the Navy required of the cache of weapons and at the same time make good on my promise to help Anthony extract his revenge.

5

MALINA

Honolulu
Four days later

I hadn't had the dream for a while, so I was due to reexperience what had happened. It was inevitable. I could try to fight it, but I felt death's fingers tugging at me throughout yesterday. And as I lay in bed in my Honolulu apartment, I'd tossed and turned in an attempt to escape the memories that invaded my consciousness without fail once or twice a month. Of course, when I fell into a more restful position, I was catapulted into the past against my will, hand in hand with my smart and sexy boyfriend Samuel, reliving those devastating hours when my world went horribly wrong at the age of seventeen.

For hours, nightmares tortured me until I sat up with a gasp, my body drenched in sweat. I curled my fingers around the thin blanket that covered me as my surroundings came into focus. I wasn't back home in Venezuela, witnessing mis padres and my boyfriend's death, but safely in my bed in Honolulu.

That day had resulted in long-term aftereffects from all I'd lost, reinforcing my inability to let people, and especially men, get close.

I tapped the screen of my phone on the bedside table. Its bright digital time reflected that I was awake in the early-morning hours—still too soon to get up for work.

Despite knowing it was a nightmare about something that had happened years before, I couldn't shake my sense of impending doom. Back then, I hadn't understood the magnitude of what we'd done by taking our grievances to the street, the repercussions of our actions in the heat of the moment, or how it would implode to affect those we loved. But Madre, Padre, and Samuel were dead, and it was my fault.

———

WORN WOODEN PLANKS from the dock cushioned my knees as a breeze stirred tendrils of my hair. Water gently lapped against the pillars of the dock and boats tethered nearby. Waxy petals from a fragrant plumeria flower rested on my open palm. The sun crested the horizon in a vibrant glow. Only a few hours old, the nightmare was fresh in my mind and made the ache of losing mis padres unbearable all over again. There was no going back, only forward. But there were times I had to put the world on pause and connect with those I'd lost. I was doing just that, claiming twilight for a few moments with mis padres and Samuel before I had to get ready for work.

As I'd done since moving there, I adopted the Hawaiian traditions over my Venezuelan ones for conformity purposes—and because they were beautiful. One that I'd borrowed was setting a lei adrift in the water when a ship went out. If the lei returned, the vessel would too. If not, all those lives would be lost in the ocean. The flower I held was chock-full of meaning. I was under no illusions that it would return to me after it was set free on the water, but it felt right to honor them in that way.

I fought a sob that lodged in my throat, wishing for the billionth time that their spirits would visit me. They never had. I missed them with every fiber of my being, and to be able to see them, to talk with them, if even only once more, would have been the greatest gift.

At least once a month, I remembered them. I let the pain of my actions come forth, mingling with all the good memories, and thanked them for saving my life. My toes pressed into the dock as I leaned forward to release the flower into the water. It was my way of memorializing them. I shifted my weight onto my heels. Tears rolled down my cheeks, and my stomach churned uneasily. *I miss you.*

Birds cried overhead, and the gentle lapping of the water against the pier helped to return harmony to my ravaged soul. I stayed as long as I was able, soaking up the natural beauty of the island.

Minutes ticked by, and I swore I felt the caress of a hand against my forehead, shifting my hair back behind my ear as Madre used to do. The breeze was mild and salt-laden, and my mind was forever wishful. As the sun began to ease its way from the ocean and into the sky, I wiped my face, loosened my grip on the threads of the past, and let the present and its day-to-day concerns seep back in.

I took in the beauty around me. My Aunt Maria and Uncle Matt—aka Mom and Dad—had been right to move us from Darien, Connecticut, that dreadful summer when I'd arrived on their doorstep. The move hadn't chased away the pain for any of us, but Hawaii was where we'd made a home. I'd found Beth, a best friend who'd accepted me even when the sense of loss was so deep I could barely breathe. Her constant upbeat chatter and infectious personality enabled me to escape my pain and get out of my head. I never told her what had happened to me—I couldn't. Later, she'd shared that her cousin had died, and that his loss had devastated her. She'd innately sensed the void that threatened to consume me and did her best to ease it.

At lunch, she'd pulled me to the table where she sat with her friends, who were nice enough. Then she'd dragged me to the movies or to hang at her house after school and often to the beach until I was able to laugh and see the world around me in color again. Her overzealous insertion into my life had been what saved me, even though she'd said I'd been the one to rescue her because her prior best friend had stabbed her in the back and dumped her. Beth wasn't the only one who'd noticed my fragile state of mind back then, even if I hadn't known it at the time. Ty had said that I'd looked haunted, and there was a lot of truth to that statement. We all were.

I'd sensed his interest back then, the way he watched over me. But I couldn't let it go anywhere, not even friendship. At that time, I desperately needed a friend and had found one in Beth. It would have been a betrayal to get close to Ty. He also reminded me of Samuel. Not in physical appearance, but in the fierce presence he had, his innate defense of those who needed it. That alone sent alarm bells through my system anytime we were within mere feet of one another, and I wanted to run as far and as fast as I could because the only thing that would follow in the wake of getting close to Ty was death.

As the sun emerged from the ocean's embrace in a blaze of reds, pinks, and oranges, I pushed to my feet, fighting a sudden bout of dizziness that was gone as quickly as it had come on. Shaking my head at the weirdness of it, I made my way back home.

I spotted Hank with his unkempt white beard, thick gray hair, and signature opened-collared Hawaiian shirt. His deep tan spoke of his love of the outdoors while he took up space under a palm tree not far from where I walked. He owned a fishing boat rental at the marina and had been there for a long time. We'd become fast friends when I'd roamed the docks aimlessly during my first summer in Honolulu. As I neared him, I gave him a little wave. "Anyone out fishing this morning?"

Broad shoulders shrugged, and he ran a hand along his thick whiskers. The lines in his face eased for a moment, defying the tiredness I saw clinging to his half-mast eyelids.

"A couple have gone out." He nodded toward the pier I'd left. "Couldn't sleep?"

He knew what I'd been doing. He had my dad's confidence after he'd found me playing hours of chess on the docks, which meant Hank knew my life story. "One of those nights."

"Me too. They're too often for my liking."

I bent and hugged him before saying goodbye. I didn't have a lot of time before work, and I wanted to make something to eat, which caused thoughts of my old life to fill my mind once more. When I was growing up, Madre and I used to make *perico vene-zolano* for breakfast. It consisted of diced tomatoes and onions mixed with scrambled eggs with a side of avocado or mango and homemade *arepas*, cornmeal pockets.

In no time at all, I was back in my apartment, taking out ingredients. Making the food was another way for me to remember, to connect. I took peace from the ritual. While I cooked the dish we'd made hundreds of times, I revisited happy memories of growing up. The infectious sound of mi madre's laughter was almost tangible, a cherished gift. Tears were close, but I held them at bay.

Mis padres had done what they thought was right for me. They'd saved me at the cost of their lives. My current mom and dad were the only people close to me who knew the burden I carried. Not even Beth knew my true origins. I'd learned to keep my own counsel. I wished I'd known better back then.

Naive to the core, I hadn't realized that my behavior would direly affect those I loved. By being a rebellious teenager, I'd sentenced my parents to death. They'd laid down their lives to sneak me out and save me.

I glanced at the clock only to realize I needed to get moving if I wanted to be at work on time. My stomach was full, and I got ready in record time, hopped into my car, and made the drive there, effectively returning my mind to the present. A part of me hoped that Ty would be back from his mission when I arrived, regardless of our prickly demeanor toward one another. Well, that was mostly from me. I rolled my eyes. He didn't help things with the movies.

Pulling into a parking space, nausea that'd plagued me the past couple of weeks returned. Despite the physical discomfort, I did my best to ignore it as I sat with the car door open.

The morning breeze carried salty air and the pungent smell of exhaust from a Humvee rumbling not far from me. The peace I felt earlier at the docks was long gone. I lifted a chunk of my heavy hair from where it clung to my perspiration-coated face and neck, fanning underneath to try to cool down. I sucked a breath through my nose and slowly exhaled out my mouth, trying to quell my temperamental stomach. At first, I'd thought I had a stomach bug but decided I should see a doctor. It wasn't going away and had been going on for too long.

I got out of my car, heaved in a careful breath, then slammed the door shut. *Why the heck am I so hot?*

With an absent click of my key fob over my shoulder to lock my car, I crossed the parking lot at Pearl Harbor's naval base on my way to work. Without a cloud overhead, it was another beautiful day in Honolulu, but I wasn't feeling it.

I swiped my hand across my forehead to clear away the dampness—*ew*. The day had to get better. The building where I worked wasn't far, which meant blessed air-conditioning was almost within reach. Mike, who headed up the treasury, was about a foot in front of me and opened the door. Unaware I was behind him, he didn't hold it, but I managed to grasp the heavy metal before it shut. With a tug, I swung it wide and stepped inside, blinking to adjust from natural light to the harsh fluorescent. A blast of cool air hit me in the face, and my eyes almost rolled back in my head from the sheer bliss of it.

I clutched the edge of the door so it wouldn't swing back and clip my heel. I turned to the side as Anna, one of the analysts, approached. She rushed toward me, and I held the door. Maybe she was going home. If so, she was lucky. That was what I wanted to do, and my day hadn't even begun.

I blinked as she got closer, sure I was seeing things. There was wildness in her gaze. She didn't say anything, but the pinched lines around her pink lipstick-stained mouth caused me to stop, alarmed by whatever had brought on her current state. She intercepted me as I crossed the threshold, clamped her hand on my arm, and squeezed to a point where I knew I would have bruises. Her big brown eyes went wide, and she waved her hand for me to back up, her gold bangle bracelets tinkling a pretty alarm.

"Ouch, Anna. What's going on?" Confused, I took a step back, the door resting at a forty-five-degree angle against my back as I stood on the cement outside. I tried to free my arm, but she had a death grip on it. The sunlight streamed through the gap and caught the diamond nose piercing she had, momentarily distracting me until I felt the bite of her fingers on my bicep tighten even more.

She shushed me and blocked the entrance with her small body, her voice a low, urgent whisper. "Go. Leave, Malina."

"What? Why?" I stood still, confusion chasing away the last of my stomach issues. *See?* I reprimanded myself. *It's mental, all in my head.* I needed to get over whatever was making me nervous. Probably Ty and his mere presence in my life. That man drove me nuts. *With want!* my traitorous mind shouted in defiance.

Her grip tightened enough that I got out of my head and

paid attention to what she was trying to tell me. She stepped closer so only an inch separated us and dropped her voice to a conspiratorial whisper. "Agents are swarming around your desk. Mark is with them. I heard talk of treason."

"I don't understand." Any levity I'd had that morning died a swift death. "I haven't done anything wrong."

Anna herded me back, her panic seeping into my stuttered steps. "Run, Lina." She gave me a shove out the door, severing my grip on the edge of it. "They think you're the mole."

Holy shit! "I'm not a traitor, Anna. I have nothing to hide."

She shook her head, her long dark hair a curtain around her shoulders. "They found something. They won't listen. You have to go."

"I didn't do anything. You have to believe me," I pleaded then pivoted on my heel and sprinted for my car. Leaving wasn't rational. I got that, but I couldn't stop the fear from licking up my spine or my flight reaction from kicking into full gear. The same emotions about how I'd left my old life plagued me. Both times, I'd had to flee in a fight for my life.

My heart slammed against my rib cage. Key fob in hand, I unlocked my car, yanked open the door, and fell inside. The engine roared to life at the press of a button. Of course, the humidity had zero effect anymore.

I fought my hair, shoving the long strands from my forehead, and tried to calm myself and think rationally. But that same feeling from when I'd left Venezuela was too deeply ingrained. I shouldn't have run, but the intense fear I had of being captured without control over my fate and Anna's frightened insistence overrode common sense. I didn't think my past and present would collide. But maybe it had. Maybe they had learned the secret my family buried. Precious seconds ticked by while I wrestled with how much trouble I could get in if they had indeed discovered the truth about me.

I shook my head, trying to clear the fear that had me in a

choke hold. They couldn't have found out. My dad would have called.

But something must have flagged this scrutiny that centered on my workstation, or they wouldn't be searching my computer or setting a trap for when I arrived. I had to do something. If I went back, it wouldn't be good. I eased off the accelerator to turn out of the lot then increased my speed.

That saying "damned if you do, damned if you don't" swirled in my frantic mind. I already looked guilty for fleeing. There had to be somewhere to go, someone to turn to for help.

That was when I thought of *him*. Ty's face swam in my mind. *No, no, no.* I cringed against the heat that followed the visualization. We had history, some of which I hadn't wanted to face, especially not the time—the morning after our only date—when I said that what'd happened between us was a mistake. In a panic, I'd told him to stay the hell away from me. It wasn't my finest moment.

At the time, I'd been deflecting my own worry over my heart because he was Tyler Hale, a god among boys in high school. A freaking legend. *Who am I kidding? He's the same now.* Panties dropped when he walked by. I huffed out a breath. I was digressing. I needed to snap out of it.

He was incredible at his job. And when it came to his team or family, he would do anything. I had to bank on the slight chance that I could be included in that very same team mentality. It was a long shot, but maybe.

If anyone would help me, he would. No matter the animosity I'd shown him for the past year. He wouldn't hold a grudge. It was just one date. I needed to let it go. Besides, Vegas hadn't ended in complete disaster, at least mostly. My mind chose that moment to allow a reminder of our gambling and alcohol-infused weekend to infiltrate, along with my denial when I'd found myself in bed with him *again*. God, the problem wasn't only him. I was weak when it came to that man.

He'd continued to pursue me. I had been the one to shut things down when I wasn't under the influence of the wild and uncontrollable attraction I had for him.

I shoved the thought away. There wasn't time to revisit that until I was safe. And there was only one place I could think of where I would be okay, his family's private island.

I knew no one would think to look for me there, especially since Ty and I appeared at work as though we couldn't stand each other on a good day. I got the irony that I thought of us as being on the same team when I was constantly pushing him away, but desperate times…

My tires squealed as I took a tight turn fast. I needed to focus, get what I needed from my place, ditch the car, then find my way to the island. He wouldn't be there. He wasn't even in Hawaii.

SEAL Team 9 had been on a mission in Venezuela. Ty's team had returned with all but one of the hostages and without him. I had to have faith that he would come home. For the time being, I couldn't think about all the reasons why, not until I was at his place and could investigate what had happened at work and how to fix it.

Please be home soon, Ty.

6

TYLER

Venezuela

The hardtop Jeep bumped over potholes in the road. The cover of night had faded and no longer shielded Anthony and me as we closed in on our destination to locate and photograph the cache of weapons that the Venezuelan government and a small but powerful militia were rumored to possess.

Before Rich and Joe left to transport the other American hostages home, Anthony had disclosed the general location of where he'd overheard the weapons were held—the city of San Antonio del Táchira, Venezuela. It was across the river from Cúcuta, Colombia, where we had experienced tragedy after receiving bad intel. Anthony also confirmed that the Mahrib Allah militia group was behind their kidnapping and involved with the weapons.

I made sure his wounds were treated and gave him food and water. We'd obtained a vehicle for the long drive from the El Palito port to an area along the war-torn Venezuelan border, which we would embark upon that night. Convincing my team to leave us behind wasn't difficult, as they wanted closure—and to find the mole in our organization. They called in extraction details and would arrange for a narrow boat to be tied under the Simón Bolívar International Bridge. That waterway would be manned by border patrol and closed for passage, but it was our best shot out. I had a tranquilizer gun in my pack that I would use on them, which would also confuse our enemies about our entry point into Colombia.

Anthony dozed on and off during the drive. We passed under a canopy of trees as we neared the nine-hundred-eighty-foot bridge, traveling on back roads as much as possible. The vehicle bounced along uneven dirt trails, and my mind flashed to Anthony's wife's lifeless body. Given the threat the SEAL team faced, I worried for Malina's safety because of her connection with me. The older generations from SEAL Team 9 were being targeted for elimination in what reeked of personal vendetta. They weren't the only ones. Wives and descendants had also been killed.

My parents had stayed on their boat, extending their vacation but moving around and only going into ports to get supplies. They'd assured us it wasn't a hardship, and they were enjoying themselves. Our dad and mom understood what we were doing without having to say anything, as he was a member of SEAL Team 9 before he retired years before. Of course, my brothers, Jaxon and Xander, and I were highly motivated to eliminate the threat so they could come home.

I nudged Anthony awake. We were getting close, and I had a few questions that needed answering. It took a few minutes for him to be alert enough to give me the information I needed.

"Where are we?" He drew a hand over his face, wincing from the action.

"Not far. What information were they trying to get from you during that interrogation?"

"I'm the guy who designed the new encryption code recently rolled out for our military records. They wanted me to access and decode military personnel files they'd stolen."

Shit. That was even more of a reason to do everything we could to stop them. We rode the next few miles in silence, and I digested who I had next to me and how unwise it was to have him anywhere where he could get detained again. A glance at his battered face and the determination he had to see things through was evident in his tense posture and the deep lines carved around his mouth.

The front tire hit a large pothole, and I slowed the Jeep. I pulled over to the side and into the surrounding vegetation. We were close. I wanted to go in on foot. "I'm going to take a look around. Stay here."

"No." He pressed his mouth into a straight line, splitting his lip back open. It started to bleed. "This is my fight, too, and I know what some of them look like."

There was that, though I didn't think it would be hard to spot them. "How are you with a gun?"

"Good enough to know how to point and shoot."

I grunted and handed a gun to him. Given to the shape of his torn and bloodstained shirt, I pulled a clean one from my pack and helped him into it. It wouldn't hide the swelling on his face or the cuts, but it was the best we could do. Rich had given Anthony a pair of boots, so he at least had something protecting his feet.

It was early enough for the area not to be too busy. Because of the state Anthony was in, I didn't hustle through the forest but took a more direct route down the dirt road so he could find his footing easier, but I could still pull him deep into the vegetation at the first sound of a vehicle.

By the time we got to a clearing near the bridge, Anthony was breathing hard, a fine sheen of sweat coating his face.

People milled about the semi-busy city but not the ones we were looking for.

"The warehouse is over there." He pointed, thumped against the building, then slid down. "I'll just wait here."

That wasn't going to work. I maneuvered him to a small café. Once in a chair, he rested his head on his arms on top of the table. The place wasn't open. "I'll be about ten to fifteen minutes."

I hurried back to where we were then peered around the corner of a run-down store. He'd pointed a few buildings over and had said he'd heard it described as a gray structure with few windows not far from the bridge. The militia soldiers' voices carried not far from where I was pressed against the back of the boarded-up bakery. I counted to five. When there was a lull and the sounds were moving away, I glanced again. The soldiers had moved another foot away, their sights blocked by the front corner of the structure.

From the back of the store, I sprinted to the rear of the building then checked windows for occupancy and wires. When I was sure there wasn't an alarm hooked up, I pried one open, climbed inside, and scrambled into an empty corner. The lights were on in the front of the open space. Crates were stacked in the middle of the oversized room.

The voices were coming from the front, so I used the stacked wooden boxes as cover. I had a bad feeling about what was in them. Even from where I crouched, I could make out some of the foreign words stamped on the side of the crates, but I didn't know what it meant. Closing the distance, I pulled the small waterproof camera from a pocket and snapped pictures, including a shot of a crowbar to one side of the pile.

I inched around then grabbed it before the men in the front moved again. I pried open one of the crates and found military-grade weapons inside. I took as many pictures as I could, pausing when I got a good look at what was nestled in the next box I opened—a nuclear weapon.

I left everything as it was, having taken more than enough pictures for evidence. We couldn't sit on this. I snuck back out. Once clear and far enough away, I sent a communication with coordinates for where the weapons were stored and uploaded the images.

As soon as I finished, a shout went out not far from where the men were. Feet pounded against the sidewalk. The sound of a fist hitting flesh carried clearly. Then I heard a voice I knew too well—Anthony.

Unfurling from my position behind the bakery, I sprinted to where I'd heard him to join the fight and hopefully get us out of a sticky situation.

7

MALINA

Honolulu

I compiled lists in my head as I raced up the stairs to my second-floor apartment. My hand shook as I tried to fit the key into the lock. On the third attempt, I got it and burst inside, my heartbeat a loud staccato in my ears. I secured the dead bolt behind me, grabbed a backpack from the hook by the door, then hurried to my desk in the living room.

I stuffed in my computer, power cords, and purse. I purposely powered off my phone and made a mental note to get a burner. Next, I rushed to my bedroom, scooped up clothes, and shoved them in. I shimmied out of my work clothes, trading them for yoga pants, a stretchy T-shirt, a nondescript hoodie, and gym shoes. With deft fingers, I twisted my hair up and out of the way, securing it into a bun. I turned in a circle. *What am I forgetting?*

With no more time, I left as quickly as I'd arrived. With my backpack straps settled over my shoulders, I locked up behind me then took the stairs to the ground floor. As I exited the apartment complex, sirens screamed as they rounded the corner. I flipped my hood up, thankful my hair was in a bun, which made me less recognizable. Head down, I trudged along the sidewalk as a bus pulled up not far ahead. At the last minute, I fell into line then boarded.

Nausea churned in my stomach, and my heart beat at an alarming rate. I wasn't home free, not yet. I fell into a lone seat and slouched down, bending in half so that my head rested over my knees and on my folded arms, hidden from the window. About a minute later, the bus rumbled away, and I pretended to sleep.

After clearing a few blocks, I sat up and looked out the window. We were headed downtown, which was perfect. I could get off close to the harbor and talk to Hank about procuring a small motorboat. I had enough cash in my purse to get what I needed at the store but would need more for the aging veteran who lived on a houseboat near the fishing-boat rentals. Thankfully, he had a soft spot for me.

Threading my fingers together, I attempted to stop them from shaking, berating myself again for having run. It made me look guilty, and I knew it. But I wasn't naive enough to think the buried details of my past that had escaped my initial back-ground check wouldn't reveal themselves under scrutiny. It was likely that they would stick me in an interrogation room and then a holding cell, all because of a past I had no control over and decisions that had been made for me. Just the thought of being confined and unable to leave under my own free will caused a layer of perspiration to coat my skin all over again. I sucked in air, forcing myself to regulate my breathing.

The bus stopped to let people off then rumbled down the street, hampered here and there by traffic. When we were close enough to where I wanted to be, I got up and exited with a fiftysomething man in worn jeans and a ratty shirt. My head was down, my face hidden by the angle of my hood. I had to be careful of cameras. Taking measured steps, I joined groups of others while walking. When the couple of older women I walked with neared a convenience store, I broke free and slipped inside. Hurrying down the aisles, I grabbed a prepaid phone and snacks. I wandered the rows, double-checking that I had what I needed. I didn't know when I could return.

I rounded the corner to the next aisle and stopped short, cold dread washing over me as bits and pieces of how I'd been feeling flooded my consciousness. *When was the last time I'd had to buy tampons?* Horror slammed me in the gut as I did the math in my head—two months ago. *Oh God, no.*

My mouth filled with saliva, and I frantically swallowed down the excess. I would not be sick in there. It had to be a miscalculation, a mistake. With shaky fingers, I grabbed a pregnancy test then rushed to the counter. I paid with the small amount of money I had on hand. If all went well on the island, I wouldn't need more. However, I did need some cash to buy a boat from Hank.

There was an ATM near the door. I ticked off all the reasons I shouldn't access my account, but I only had five dollars left. I had to risk it but did my best to keep my face shadowed and angled away from the camera, which didn't mean all that much, as they would be able to trace my electronic transactions. I shoved my debit card into the chip reader, punched in my four-digit passcode, withdrew the max-allowed amount from the ATM, then secured the stack of cash in my backpack with the debit card I couldn't use again.

With the plastic bag secured on my wrist and my hands back in the front pocket of my hoodie, I rejoined the morning foot traffic on the sidewalk. Most folks seemed to be heading to work, but I made a beeline for the harbor. Freedom was so very close. I could almost feel it despite the bitter taste of fear.

I hovered close to crowds, blending in with them and staying under awnings to keep myself off cameras. Fifteen minutes passed and then half an hour, until the air was thick with salt from the ocean. I knew of a couple of motorboats I could rent.

Hank was an old, cantankerous man who lived aboard his houseboat, but I had a few hundred dollars in my purse, enough to buy one of the dented boats off him.

My whole time in Hawaii, I'd known him to hang around the harbor, even as I was lost in my own grief. He'd been the one person who'd understood and given me what I needed to survive. Our friendship began when he asked me to play chess one day and had grown from there. When I showed promise with strategy, he shifted focus and tutored me, providing an education about things I never would have learned in school, such as the dark web, hacking, and military strategy. He and my dad had close ties, and because of their mutual respect and my frequent trips to the marina, Hank was privy to why I was in Hawaii and could never return to where I'd come from. But those memories were better to languish in when I was away from there.

I spotted him where he usually sat during the day, in the shade of a palm tree, eyes closed as if he was napping. I stopped in front of him, and when he didn't immediately open his eyes, I toed the bottom of his flip-flop, whispering his name.

A smile curved his craggy, whiskered face. "What are you doin', girlie? Playing hooky?"

Normally, I would have rolled my eyes and given him crap for the way he greeted me but not today. "I'm in a bit of trouble."

Awareness filtered into his dark eyes, and he leveled me with a steely glare. "What ya need?"

I peeled off two hundred, bent, and pressed the bills into his weathered hand. "A motorboat. An older one that won't be missed. And your silence on the matter."

Frown lines deepened. "As if you'd need to ask." He pocketed the cash then pointed to a banged-up boat at the end of a line of several others that made up his casual fishing-boat-rental business. "It's gassed up. I never saw ya."

"Thanks, Hank. When everything's clear, I'll be back."

"You let me know if you need anything, girlie."

I rolled my eyes, desperate for some levity. "It's all bogus, but I can't risk staying right now."

"Your folks know?"

I shook my head. "Soon." I gave him a quick hug then straightened and pivoted toward the boats. I untied the skiff and climbed aboard. I glanced at Hank, who appeared to be sleeping again. But I knew better. The old vet was on full alert. He was as loyal as they came, just not to the powers that be, who'd abandoned him upon his return to civilization. Special Forces to the core, he'd had his hands in more government cover-ups and intel than the general public would ever know about.

I hurried to the boat he'd referenced and got to work with the next phase of my plan—hiding out on Ty's island.

I stowed the backpack under the seat with the plastic bag from the convenience store safely inside, untied the skiff, and got the engine purring. With one hand on the tiller of the outboard motor and the other on the side of the small vessel, I headed through the no-wake zone and toward open waters.

I glanced behind me one last time, scanning the docks to make sure I hadn't been followed and that the police weren't hassling Hank. Three men strolled along the boardwalk, and my gaze skimmed over them until something nagged in the back of my mind, and I jerked my eyes back. *I know him.* The guy closest to the water was familiar in the way he walked, his hawk-like features, his tall slim build, his overconfident swagger, the way his hair fell across his forehead, and the pointy chin. He had been one of the people around my family in Venezuela, and he was not a good man.

If he was here, that meant… I couldn't think about it. It must have been a mistake. It couldn't have had anything to do with me. Dad and I had been over it time and again, and he'd reassured me that to those men, I no longer existed. I had to call him.

There was nothing I could do but move forward, and I turned to face away from the harbor, focusing on my escape rather than what-ifs. I had a general enough idea of where I had to go to get to the private island. The key was to avoid any boats so no one could report seeing a lone figure in a hoodie with no fishing gear in sight.

It took longer than it should have to spot the island in question, but I'd had to take a roundabout way there to minimize the risk. A slightly altered course meant my approach was along a heavily vegetative section. With the small boat, I was able to get close to the shore before cutting the engine and tilting it so the outboard motor wouldn't get damaged when I dragged it into the trees for cover. The boat couldn't be visible from the ocean or the air. I stripped off my shoes and socks, shoved them into my pack, and secured it on my back once more. My yoga pants were pulled up to my knees so they wouldn't get wet.

Jumping into the shallow water, I took hold of the small motorboat, guiding it to the shore with me. When the bottom grounded against the sand, I prepared for the very difficult job of dragging the aluminum boat to the forest line. While it was fairly lightweight, it was bulky and grated against the wet sand as I pulled for all I was worth. Sweat poured down my face and trickled under the thick sweatshirt. I took a moment to peel the clothing off then dropped it into the boat for the time being.

Hiding the boat took longer than I'd expected, and a raging thirst took hold of me once I was satisfied with the camouflage job I'd done to cover the skiff with fronds. I'd hidden it between the bushes beneath the canopy of palms. I went back to shore and gathered a handful of shells to leave at the base of one of the palms at the edge of the forest line to help me find the boat if I was in a hurry.

Even though I didn't think anyone was there, I would be careful. Ty and I had talked briefly about his brother Xander getting married, and that he was on his honeymoon. I thought they had another week until their three-week vacation was over. Then they'd be back permanently. I didn't know where Jaxon was, but I hoped he, too, wasn't in residence. It was a huge risk I had to take. Worst-case scenario, I could hide out in the middle of their island and sleep outside. There were plenty of fruit trees, and I could steal a fishing rod when no one was paying attention. It could work.

I jogged along the edge of the vegetation, hoping to minimize being spotted if anyone was there. It didn't take long until I came upon the four houses. I had intimate knowledge of the one on the end, Tyler's. I'd been there once, a year ago, and it had been enough to leave a lasting impression.

The beach in front of the houses looked undisturbed. There were no footprints, nothing to indicate anyone was there. I hurried up a few steps and entered the lanai. The door was unlocked. I wasn't as lucky with the main entrance to the house. I pulled two bobby pins from my hair, stripped off the rubber ends, bent them each to a ninety-degree angle, and got to work on the lock. When the tumblers responded and the dead bolt slid back, a rush of success washed over me.

I was in. I viewed the open-concept beach house where I would mount a case for my defense, hacking my way into systems to gather the information I would need—well, maybe. I was still a little iffy about doing that.

My heart slowed to a manageable rhythm, and I glanced around the interior. A part of me melted at being in Ty's home, sensing his powerful presence in the space and wanting to wrap myself in the safety it offered. I could breathe again.

But it wasn't long before the reality of my situation came

crashing to the forefront. Until Ty came home, I only had myself to rely on. I stripped off my pack and set it on the table. I was once again in a fight for my life. As if suspicion of treason wasn't bad enough, the presence of Venezuelan militia felt like the final nail in my coffin.

8

TYLER

Venezuela

I burst forward to find Anthony on his knees with a gun pressed to his forehead. With my own weapon extended, I shot the man looming over him in the forehead then eliminated the target across from me with a hit to the chest then the head. To the right, I fired the same shots. I swung to the left as the butt of a gun crashed into my temple. Stars burst behind my eyes, and the world went dark.

When I came to, my hands were zip-tied, and someone was dragging me by the foot. My head thumped over a clump of dirt. I counted at least two men aside from the one who was pulling me toward the building. But there would be more.

I couldn't see Anthony. With my unencumbered leg, I kicked out, striking the guy who had hold of my leg in his wrist. A crack sounded, and he screamed. I lunged to the side as the butt of a machine gun narrowly missed my head. Rolling to my feet, I threw my weight to the other side, forcing the insurgent to my right off-balance. I brought my bound hands to my mouth, clamped my teeth on the end of the plastic, tightened the ties, then slammed them down over a raised knee. The plastic snapped.

Another of the men aimed his weapon, and I ducked then swept his legs out from under him. As I lurched to my feet, another attacked. Using his arm for momentum, I slammed him into the side of the building they were dragging me into. I raised my elbow behind me, sinking it into the soldier at my back. He stumbled, and I followed with a fist to his face. We went down with my hands wrapped around his neck. I caught movement to my side and reacted. One hand stayed on the guy's neck, cutting off his air, and I swept up his firearm.

The last soldier was using Anthony as a shield and pressing a gun to his temple. I squeezed the trigger. The bullet found a home in the soldier's forehead, knocking his head back. His arm went slack, and Anthony stumbled to the side. I was on my feet in a heartbeat and tightly gripped Anthony's arm. We had to get out of there.

He jerked free, bent, and retrieved the dead man's gun. One after another, he drilled holes in the corpse until the clip was empty. Then he kicked him in the ribs.

I had to pull him away. "He's dead."

"He was the one who brought my wife and tortured her." One more kick landed to the side of the dead man's head before he let me lead him away. That must have been why he'd left the safety of his table—he'd seen that man. I couldn't fault him for that.

I retrieved my bag from where one of the insurgents had dropped it, along with several weapons.

Anthony stumbled after me as I half dragged him toward the back of the buildings and in the direction of the river. We weren't far. When there was enough distance, I pulled a knife from my bag. As it was, one of my guns was gone.

After I cut the zip ties from his bound hands, Anthony was able to keep up a little better. Beneath the bridge ahead was the boat my team had arranged. When we were in range, I used the tranquilizer gun to neutralize the border guards, and we hurried to where the longboat was tethered.

There were clothes in the boat, a hat, and an empty bottle of tequila that would help to explain Anthony's hazy state if we were caught. I helped him remove his stained and torn shirt and change into yet another tan T-shirt then plopped the wide-brimmed hat on his head. I steadied the boat, and he got in. Once seated, he picked up an oar.

The adrenaline from our escape was wearing off, and I could see the toll it had taken on his battered body and soul as exhaustion appeared to take hold of him. "Focus on me." I waited until his eyes cleared enough to pay attention. "Hang on tight to the oar and make the motions through the water without taxing yourself. I'll be beneath the boat, moving it along. It would help our disguise, just for the stretch near the building and just past it, if you could drunkenly slur the words to a popular song from here but not too loud."

He nodded, and I paused for half a second to make sure the next part sunk in. "If there's trouble, stomp once on the boat. I'll surface and take care of it."

The bed of the river wasn't deep close to the edge. When it did drop in depth, we would be far enough downriver for me to climb in and take over the rowing. He dipped the oar in the water, and I slipped beneath the murky river water.

Once under, I gripped the bottom of the boat and walked along the bank, staying close to the side of the river and moving us away from the threat. I could hear Anthony's wobbly voice belting out a song in half Spanish, half humming. The boat rocked side to side every once in a while. He wouldn't last much longer before passing out, but he was hanging in there as best he could. His wavering would make him appear to a casual observer as if he was drunk. It was convincing.

Every fifteen minutes, I surfaced enough to draw air before ducking back under. We traveled at a moderate pace, doing what we could not to draw attention. When we were far enough away, I surfaced and took stock of our surroundings. Thick forest blanketed us on either side. I motioned for Anthony to put the oar in the boat then climbed inside. We weren't far from the extraction point. A blanket of humidity hung in the air, and the natural sounds of birds and monkeys indicated people weren't closing in on us.

I took the oar from Anthony, and he slumped forward, resting his head on bent arms. I could carry him the short way through the jungle, and we would probably get there sooner if I did.

We traveled another mile downriver before I maneuvered us to a small bank. The thick odor of rotting vegetation permeated the air. We had under an hour to make it to the extraction point. I hopped out, and my boots suctioned to the muddy riverbed, fighting against me while I dragged the skit into the underbrush.

Anthony was out cold. I swung him over my shoulder in a fireman's carry, and we were on our way. I wove around the jungle's densely tangled branches and leaves, taking care to step over exposed roots.

Even maintaining vigilance of our guerrilla-insurgent-infested jungle surroundings, the terror of what Anthony had endured with his wife's murder topped our present danger. His loss, her lifeless, bruised, and bloody body, brought home with crystal clarity the conversation I needed to have with Malina about what had happened between us in Vegas. Life was too unpredictable to keep playing games with the woman I wanted to spend the rest of my life with.

9

MALINA

Private Island in Hawaii

After two full glasses of water, I sat at the kitchen table and drummed my fingers on the rectangular surface, waiting for the adrenaline to wear off. It was both comforting and unsettling to be in Tyler's beach house. The fact that he wasn't back from the latest mission was worrisome, but at least I could crash there, and so far, his brothers weren't around.

As the minutes ticked by, the gravity of what I'd done hit home. I wasn't guilty, not of everything. But I'd run, which probably solidified to the powers that be that I was. I dropped my head into my hands. *I'm so screwed.*

I thought about everything that had happened, the events that landed me there. I'd done what Padre had said and given Dad, my uncle Matt, the locket with the tiny flash drive. As he said, the small device had bought me freedom and buried the records about my true identity. And while I hadn't committed treason, I was guilty of withholding information about where I was born. The government would surely discover my secret in the meticulous investigation they would conduct, even if I was being falsely accused. I would work remotely to clear my name.

My fingers drummed a frustrated beat against the wood. *Why had Mark been at my desk—helping the agents?* That didn't sit right and added another piece to the puzzle I would scrutinize as soon as I took some time to get myself under control.

I couldn't put it off any longer. I had to call my dad. Even though his title as "Dad" had been a cover, in a way, he and Mom had become my parents.

I glanced at the time and realized that he would be at work. I tapped the numbers I knew by heart onto the burner phone's screen then waited for him to pick up. I'd bypassed his secretary, using a direct line he'd made me commit to memory.

The sound of his voice washed over me, and I had to bite my lip to keep from crying. He'd been my rock when I'd needed him most. "Hey, Dad. I'm in trouble."

"What? Where are you?" His voice cracked like a whip through the speaker.

I cringed. It wasn't the best way to start a conversation. "I'm safe." I went into detail about what Anna had told me, how I'd fled, and finally, about the men at the marina.

"You're sure they didn't see you?" Worry laced his words.

"Positive. But I'm worried they found me somehow."

"As far as the world is concerned, you are Malina. Any other records were buried with a clearance few could access."

I huffed out a nervous breath. We'd been over it so many times when I was younger. Nothing had happened, not until now, and I had to believe it was a coincidence.

"We'll fix this." His confidence and determination bled through the phone, washing over me with unconditional love. "Stay where you are. Don't make any other calls. I'll text you with a burner number when I get it. We can communicate that way after I do some digging."

Panic stabbed me in the gut. "No, Dad. Please don't do any digging. It'll only alert the government that you've talked to me. Can you and Mom go on a vacation for a week or so?"

"I don't want to leave you, Lina. She won't either."

My heart melted. They'd rallied around me and given me protection when I'd needed it most. I couldn't lose them, not again, not given how I'd lost Madre and Padre. "You're not leaving me. But I want you safe, and those men—"

"Are anything but." Dad sighed, his resignation heavy between us even across the distance. "I don't have court anytime soon. I can work remotely, and your mom would love to get away. She can ask another pediatrician in her office to cover for her. But only if you stay hidden. We'll come up with a plan when I get another phone."

I assured him I would, and that I would have help when Tyler arrived. That part was a fib, but I wanted them safe and not to do anything foolish. If those men at the marina got to them, I would lose another set of parents. I didn't think I could survive a second tragedy of that measure.

I stood from the table, curious to know more about Tyler while I wasn't distracted by his larger-than-life presence. I understood why my best friend, Beth, had fallen for him in high school. And why he liked her—she had blue eyes, long strawberry-blond hair, and curves for days. Despite her knockout looks, she was the sweetest person I'd ever met. She'd been my physics lab partner when I enrolled in high school in Honolulu my senior year, and we'd hit it off from the start.

She and Tyler had gotten together shortly after I'd moved there. It didn't last. None of his short-term girlfriends did, if they could even be called that. He hadn't ever said they were exclusive or that they were anything more than they were. There had been an elusiveness about him back then, an unwillingness to commit. In fact, he'd told her he didn't want a girlfriend. But those three days had been enough for Beth to fall hard and then have her heart shattered. Our new friendship had weathered that particular storm, initiating me into best friend status overnight. I'd needed a friend then too.

We'd made a pact when he broke her heart never to go out with guys like him, the super-hot, love-'em-and-leave-'em type, the guys who were not relationship material. It was a rule I'd broken almost a year before when I'd gone on a date with Tyler.

The guilt when I'd woken and thought of Samuel and the fragmented state of my heart, of the harm I couldn't let befall another by entering into a serious relationship with me, had been staggering. Of course, I'd pushed him away, and Ty and I had become more frenemies than anything else.

I didn't have many friends aside from Anna and Beth. Hooking up with Tyler had felt like a betrayal to Beth. I didn't let many people in, but I had with her. The fear of losing her friendship over a broken pact, a violated girl code, had reared its juvenile head, and I couldn't use adult logic to squelch it. So I'd done what came naturally to me and ran.

But honestly, that wasn't what had driven me from his arms. It was how much I'd loved Samuel, the last text from him, and knowing his death was on me.

I used the girl pact in my mind to trick myself into believing the problem stemmed from that as opposed to any deep-seated tragedy. Over the years, Beth and I had stayed in touch. She'd gone away to college and met Dan. They got married and lived in California with their two kids. I missed her but was glad she was happy. Her happiness made my worry over a broken pact seem silly, but I went with it. That way, I didn't have to process where the guilt was coming from.

Anna had become a good friend, too, but she didn't know me when we were younger and wouldn't have understood my odd mood swings the way Beth would have. She'd seen me drowning and had never pushed me to explain. Like a true friend, she'd stayed by my side, grabbed my hand, and did everything she could to keep my head above water.

No one had been able to come close to replacing Beth. She was more like a sister. We shared everything, the good times and the bad—well, everything except the unbelievable night I'd had with Tyler. The pressure was intense, and I couldn't keep the secret. I had enough that had to stay hidden as it was. The Ty story had needed to come out.

When I'd told her, she was worried, rightfully so. My heart was on the verge of falling for him, the humpty-dumpty effect soon to follow if I didn't throw up every wall I could to keep him away. Besides, he drove me nuts at work by setting his empty coffee mug and all kinds of other things, such as the DVDs, on my desk then walking away. When I confronted him about not using my office space as his dumping ground, he would ruffle my hair and tell me how cute I looked when angry, or that it was an excuse to come back to see me.

I'd needed Beth to keep me sane when it came to him. She'd talked me off the ledge, but I'd found myself right back there after that night in Vegas. I still fought the urge to call her, but I couldn't get her involved. Too much was at stake.

I tugged at the bottom of my T-shirt, my anxiety bubbling and hissing out of control. I shouldn't have been on the island, but I felt like I had no other choice. Ty was dangerous to my sanity. I couldn't seem to stay out of his bed when we were alone, which was why I'd only put myself in that situation twice, and the second time hadn't been my doing. But he was my only hope at fixing the mess I found myself in. Professionally, I trusted him. Personally, he was lethal to my very existence, and I wanted to beat him over the head more often than not.

Tired of dwelling on it, I snooped around his space a little. I wandered around the living room, noting the beachy color scheme and the new backsplash and quartz counters in the kitchen. I peeked in drawers just to see what he had in them but didn't find anything too personal. I left his stuff in the bathroom alone. Renovations had been done since the time I'd been there, and I liked his choices.

I opened a cabinet near the entertainment unit, expecting to find a slew of romantic comedies but finding none. I guessed it wasn't a secret passion that he'd passed off as gag gifts to me.

A handful of framed pictures of his family flanked the large flat-screen TV, including one of Xander and his new wife, Riley. The picture was taken on the beach outside. They were laughing, with her hair blowing in the wind and Xander's arms wrapped around her. I hadn't met her, but she was beautiful with long dark hair, arresting light eyes, and fantastic bone structure. They looked happy.

I traced my finger over Ty's face in another photo, and a deep longing caused me to sway. An image of waking in his arms invaded my mind, and I sank to the couch, letting myself go back to the weekend we'd gone to Los Vegas with Anna to celebrate Mark's birthday.

Dinner had been fun, with Anna buffering me from Ty, and I'd been glad to be there with her. From there, we'd gone directly to the gaming floor, and avoiding him was a problem. We stood next to one another while Mark gambled at the crap table. I couldn't take it. Ty's overbearing presence lit up every nerve in my body, in both good and bad ways. He was the anti-boyfriend, of the type that Beth and I swore never to get involved with—no players, no hearts broken. *No one I could love too deeply.*

I wasn't sure how much of a heart I had left. A good chunk of it was buried back in Venezuela.

I'd violated that promise once, almost a year ago, but in all fairness, I hadn't had any expectations of it going anywhere. When he'd asked if I wanted to go to a club, I'd given in because the idea of dancing against his very hard body was too much for me to resist, and it would be dark in there. I could hide how much I wanted him. With the heart-thumping music playing, I would be safe, so I gave in. As the night wore on, we'd ended up back at his beach house, and I'd slept with him.

No one had ever made me feel what he had that night. It both scared and awed me. But true to form, it was a one-night stand. Thank God I hadn't let my heart get involved.

Then there was Vegas, with its flashing lights and the high from Mark's consecutive wins saturating the air. It had messed with my mind. Ty and I had been bickering. I could never understand if our snark was from intense dislike or the raging sexual attraction that simmered beneath the veiled comments.

He could make me so mad. One conversation that night stood out, when Ty and I were side by side at the crap table. I fell into the memory, letting it take me back to that night.

"You take up too much room." I shoved him, needing more space so I could breathe. "Move over."

"You're pint-sized. Besides, if I left you alone, who knows what would happen?"

"I'm five foot four, that's hardly pint-sized, you jerk."

He rolled his eyes. "Your head barely reaches my shoulder. Pint-sized fits."

I smacked said shoulder for good measure, causing a deep laugh to rumble from his chest. I had to suppress a shiver from the effect of it. But Ty wasn't done, and I braced myself against the next outrageous comment.

"Case in point, you've got that unexpected viper tongue, and if you unleash it on one of these unsuspecting idiots who think they might have a chance with you, I'd have to get into a fight." His large hand gripped my hip then slid around, coming dangerously close to cupping my ass.

My mouth hung open. His words dripped with feigned annoyance that contrasted with his dilating pupils, and I wondered briefly if he was trying to convince himself he was doing me a favor rather than wanting to be near me. He hadn't complained about my height or "viper tongue" when we'd slept together a year before, but that was before I told him we were a mistake. I'd caught him staring at me plenty of times at work since then but couldn't give in.

"Guys!" Anna interjected, a smile in her voice. "I can feel the tension radiating over here. Is there something else going on between you two?"

Heat flooded my face. She was too close to home on that one. I mumbled how he wasn't my type—*lies*—and there was no way I was going to be another notch on his bedpost—*again*. I couldn't take it and told him I was going to try my luck at the slots. His grip tightened, and I heard his comment to Mark, which was not what I was trying to initiate: "Hey, man. Lina wants to try her hand at the nickel slots. Since trouble follows this one, I'm going to go with to keep an eye on her."

Yeah, trouble did follow me—him! I cracked my hand against the solid muscle in Ty's bicep. He didn't even flinch. "You're such an ass." I frowned, trying hard to control my barely banked fury. It was that or jump him. I had to stick with anger.

With a sharp elbow, I jabbed Ty so he would move the heck out of my way. I glared at him as he chuckled before giving Mark a quick hug. "Happy birthday." I hugged Anna, too, then reluctantly moved back to where Ty was. "Thanks for inviting us, Anna. This was fun."

Ty pulled me against him by wrapping his arm around me, his hand resting on my hip. Heat sizzled along every inch of my body where he made contact. I needed a drink. He must have felt the same, as he flagged down a waitress who was way too interested in him. Of course.

With our drink orders placed, we sidled up to the nickel slots. He left my side for a few minutes then returned with a cup full of change. I thanked him, feeling like a petulant child. I couldn't handle the pendulum sway of my emotions when he was near.

He didn't pay the overeager waitresses any attention. His focus was all on me. I nibbled on my lip, curiosity getting the better of me. "Have you watched all those romantic comedies?"

He laughed. "Yeah."

My grin was evil.

He held up his hand to stop what I was going to say. "It's not what you think. My mom loves them, and even though she only has boys, she would ask us to watch them with her. Since Xander is the most laid-back, he always did. That got Jax and me out of it, but I wanted to spend time with her doing something she loved, so I'd try to hang with her for as many as I could."

That was sweet, and I couldn't help but soften toward him. I assumed he'd been taking jabs at me when he gave me the DVDs, but maybe it wasn't like that at all. "Okay, then tell me what the reason is behind you giving me one of the movies you did. Or was it strictly because you thought I'd like watching them?"

His eyes sparkled with mirth. "A little of both. Take *How to Lose a Guy in 10 Days*. She does everything she can to make him dump her."

"And the bet?" Annoyance swirled. He'd better not have done something like that over me.

"Aside from that. Focus on her part. He fell for her, despite how much she tried to push him away. That was the message I wanted you to take from it."

Huh. I shifted from foot to foot, unsure how to respond. Instead, I fed the machine, and soon, our drinks had arrived. We chatted, and I fought the attraction by plying myself with the alcohol he readily provided. From there, the night was a blur. I couldn't remember anything except waking up sprawled over his chest, our legs twined together, naked.

I sucked in a breath as the island home came back in focus. I lurched to my feet, desperate to distract myself from how I'd woken in Ty's hotel room after having spent the night with him, not remembering a goddamned thing about it. What a waste.

I'd had enough. When more images tried to invade my stubborn brain, I couldn't handle them. Instead, I left the disturbing pictures locked in a box in my mind and made my way into one of the bedrooms, possibly his, as it was familiar and big enough to be a master, complete with an en suite bathroom. I scanned the room. It was definitely where I'd awoken after our first date. I grinned. Fitting that I made that room mine.

I fell onto the bed, fully clothed, and hugged one of the pillows to my chest. Exhaustion beat at me. I inhaled the masculine scent that clung to the pillow even after all the days Ty had been away. I was hopeless when it came to him. But the reassuring smell was enough to give me a false sense of safety, and I let myself drift off to sleep, needing a nap to deal with the remainder of the shit show that was my life and the computer hacking I would have to do to figure out how to clear my name.

1 0

TYLER

Honolulu

The extraction went seamlessly, and after Anthony and I were examined at the military hospital, I was released, while he remained for observation. I stood in the conference room, and I couldn't wait to go home and pass out after being awake for so long. The debrief took longer than I'd thought it would. But I'd answered all their questions to the best of my knowledge and delivered Anthony back to the States. The weapons location had been called in and a team sent to recover them. If I could have, I would have set a charge, but there were nukes, and that was a fallout I couldn't risk.

Daryl, our SEAL team lead, and I were finishing up before I took off for my family's island. I had two weeks of R & R starting the next day, and I needed it. When I was finally released, I headed through the office, and my gaze automatically went to where Lina sat. She wasn't there, which wasn't unusual, but her computer screen was dark. *Is she out sick?*

"Good to have you back." Mark slapped me on the back as I passed his workstation.

"Thanks." I grinned. "How are things?"

Mark glanced at Anna, who was openly staring at him as she walked back to her desk, a steaming mug of tea in her hand. The connection they had sparked and crackled through the office as his gaze followed her every move. "Good."

He was distracted, and while I was happy for him, I needed to know about Malina. "Hey, where's Lina?" I had a bad feeling in my gut. I hoped she hadn't quit.

"Shit." His face shuttered, and anger bracketed his mouth. "Not here. She's the mole."

I took a step back. "What are you talking about?" I knew the woman, and there was no way she would have committed treason. "There's no way she's the leak."

The chair squeaked as he took a seat and leaned back. "It's true. There were agents here, going over her computer, and they found an email. I helped to trace its source to Venezuela. She was communicating with someone named Hashem."

I had to talk to her and find out what really happened. There was animosity between us more often than not, but it wasn't anything malicious. She would never have put any of us at risk like that. I would have sensed it in her. "Where did they take her?"

Mark shook his head, his hand rubbed over his trim beard. "That's the thing that makes it even worse. She never showed up. Skipped town, in fact."

"They went to her apartment?" Of course they had. A security breach of such magnitude would warrant a manhunt.

"Yeah." Mark picked up a stress ball and tossed it from hand to hand. "I never would have suspected her. It's weird, but there was an electronic trail, which makes it hard to dismiss."

"Hmm. That's... odd." I rapped my knuckles on the corner of

his desk. "All right, I'm outta here for a couple of weeks. When I get back, we should go shoot some hoops or something."

"Sounds like a plan." Mark grinned then buried himself back in work as I stepped away.

63

11

MALINA

The sun was high in the sky, the air thick with humidity. The sparkling water called to me, and I couldn't resist spending time on the beach. Sunglasses on, I sat on a towel on Ty's beach in a teal bikini while frothy waves broke inches from my feet, rearranging the shore with each pass.

I should have been inside and on my laptop, trying to figure out what happened and how I'd come to be the scapegoat for all that had gone wrong with the SEAL's past missions—we'd lost lives with the leaked intel. It was a priority. The way to do that meant hacking, and I worried over the consequences. If Ty showed up soon, I could share my concerns and suspicions with him, and we could figure out a plan of attack together.

Instead of doing anything noteworthy to find the real suspect, I was sitting on the beach, baking in the sun, while other distractions that I hadn't let myself dwell on before kept my mind occupied—specifically, the reason for a certain test I needed to take.

I kicked myself for not being able to remember more of the night Ty and I had spent together in Vegas. It was bad enough that I'd awoken in that big bed in a room that was not my own, sprawled across a very naked man. A full-body shiver shook me, despite how hot it was on the beach.

Tilting my head into the warmth of the sun, I let the memories of what I did recall wash over me in a desperate search for clues, because I feared there was more to the night that eluded me.

The red felt on the crap table swam into focus behind my closed eyelids as I pictured the last conversation I'd had with Anna, my friend and Mark's girlfriend. Mark had been winning, and there was a buzz of excitement in the air, typical of Vegas. But I didn't want to stand around and watch him play any longer. We'd been at that for hours, and the crap table didn't hold an allure for me. The nickel slots were another story.

Part of me had loved that Ty wanted to make sure no one messed with me, but the other side was super irritated by his teasing words. He was trying to get under my skin to make me react and fight with him. It always worked. I swear he got a high off getting a rise out of me.

I found the machine I wanted to play, and he went away then returned with a cup full of nickels. The waitresses swarmed around him, and it irritated me, though I couldn't blame them. He was gorgeous with his powerful presence and Hawaiian heritage—sun-kissed caramel skin, dark, sinful eyes, a square jaw, and a body that promised hours of heaven… something I had intimate knowledge of.

My toes dug deeper into the sand as I lost myself to the murky depths of my prior drunken stupor and what I could recall. More waitresses came along with their suggestive smiles and trays full of beverages. Annoyed by all the attention he was getting, I downed several drinks faster than I should have. I pulled the handle for the next hour, watching the symbols on the wheel spin, which vied with the cartwheels in my head. I went for another nickel but found the cup empty. Ty took it from my hand and set it on top of the machine before leading me off the game floor and into a dark nightclub with pumping music and a kaleidoscope of flashing lights. I'd willingly followed my own personal Pied Piper in the club, where we passed hours dancing and laughing. It was the most fun I'd had in a long time.

The drinks flowed. I vaguely remembered a slow song and falling into his capable arms as we swayed together on the dance floor. Pressed against him like that… there were very few things that could compare. That was where things got hazy. I couldn't remember much from that point until waking in his embrace the next morning with a wicked hangover.

I lay down on the towel, stretching my feet so that the water washed over them in a soothing back-and-forth. That was when another piece of the puzzle revealed itself, unlocking in an overwhelming tidal wave of lust. In the early morning hours, sheets had tangled around our legs as I writhed against him.

He moved over me, devastatingly handsome and sexy as hell. My body was a slave to his every whim. He lifted me into his arms, so I was sitting astride when he thrust deep. He held me as my back arched, and my head fell back, reveling in the building desire, the unquenchable need for him. Sensations built as he moved inside me, playing my body like a fine-tuned instrument. Every place he caressed took me impossibly higher until he dipped his fingers to rub that highly sensitive nub. Thrusting deep, he toyed with me until every synapse in my body fired at once in a dazzling display of lights and blinding passion. He took me over the edge, only following after I screamed his name.

We collapsed on the bed in a tangle of limbs. Our breaths mingled. Then he slid his hand along my thigh to settle at my waist, and I whimpered. Desire built all over again. His response was immediate. He took my lips with his and kissed the breath from me. My head spun, and I threaded my fingers in his silky dark-brown hair. Skin on skin, I burned for him.

Gasping, I ruthlessly forced myself to sit up, shoving the memory of being in Ty's arms away. I was panting, my skin overly sensitive as the beach came back in focus, replacing the decadent feel of soft sheet and Ty's hard body.

My face was flushed, and my body hummed from the visualization of our night and his touch. It was one night. It didn't mean anything. But in the dark recess of my mind, I feared it meant a great deal more. I only hoped that when—if—every moment returned to me, I wouldn't have more to worry about. Because I already had a feeling that those stolen hours had given me something that would change the trajectory of my life forever.

I pushed up from the towel then grabbed it to hang over a chair on the patio. I couldn't keep putting off the inevitable. The door to the screened-in porch slammed shut behind me with the echo of an omen. My backpack was in the room—*his room*—where I'd decided to sleep. It was time. I dug around inside then pulled out the pregnancy test I'd bought at the store before leaving Honolulu.

Huffing out a breath, I went into the bathroom, giving myself a pep talk the entire time I read the directions, peed on the stick, and left it on the counter. Nausea churned in my gut as I paced in front of the wall of windows that overlooked the ocean. It was safer there, farther away. I stole another longing glance out the windows. I would rather have been swimming, on the beach, anything but waiting to see the results of one night. Three minutes had never seemed so long.

It was his fault. I pivoted, completing another rotation, and resumed my trek before the windows. That wasn't true. It took two, and I had been more than willing. An onslaught of images of Ty and the feeling of his arms around me invaded my head. A blast of heat followed, along with the burn of desire. Damn that man. He was my kryptonite.

My fingers were curled around my phone and leeched of

color in a too-tight grip. Angling it toward me, I checked the timer I'd set—only seconds to go. A wash of both fear and hope rushed through me, and I lingered on the positive of the two emotions. *Do I want a baby?*

My restless feet paused, and I let the idea of a little boy or girl solidify, imagining endless hours at the beach, playing in the sand and swimming, and that peal of joyful laughter from a child that warms your heart. I bit down on my bottom lip, coming to terms with what I wanted. *Yeah, I can do this.*

The alarm blared in the silence, shattering my daydream. My hand jerked, and the phone clattered to the floor. I swiped at the perspiration along my hairline and shut the noise off before making my way to the master bathroom. The inert stick sat on the counter, and I approached it like a bomb was about to go off. *This is it.* One peek, and I would know if my future was to take another turn.

I took a deep breath then looked—two bold lines. My hand shot out and gripped the sink as a wave of dizziness washed over me. There was no mistaking what that meant, but I grabbed the box and reread the directions just in case I was wrong. I wasn't. I was pregnant. *What the hell am I going to do?*

My fingers curled around the test, and I lifted it from the counter, taking it with me as I left the bathroom to collapse on one of the kitchen chairs. After another glance at the very pink lines, I dropped it into my purse. I knew I would want to look again later, as it didn't seem real yet.

I could feel shock settling in, and I shivered in the cool air-conditioning. I couldn't stay inside. The walls were closing in on the heels of my discovery. I had to get out of here. Needing the warmth of the sun, the hypnotic sound of the waves as they rolled and broke along the shore, I grabbed a dry towel and a water bottle. The screen door to the porch slammed behind me, and my toes curled in the soft sand. I let the smell of salty air spiced with hibiscus and coconuts wash over me.

The closer I got to the water's edge, the more determined I became to figure out what to do about my current predicament because it wasn't just my life anymore. I would fight with every fiber of my being to clear my name and give my child the future he or she deserved.

12

MALINA

It was peaceful on the island. The day was long, and as dusk approached, I had trouble keeping my eyes open. I had a sandwich for dinner, and I wiped down the kitchen before going into Ty's room to change into sleep shorts and a top. Thankfully, I had my iPad and planned to read on the patio until I was tired enough to sleep.

The news I'd learned earlier was enough of a shock that I needed to indulge in some lazy beach time and reading. And I had. Tomorrow was a new day, and I would tackle what I could of my problems then.

I sensed the change in the atmosphere, not even two steps out of his room, as if the space had shrunk. A heady sense of anticipation tiptoed along my body.

"Malina?"

Ty stood before me, weary but larger than life and representing the possibility of a buoy in a raging sea. The multifaceted question imbedded in the way he said my name drew me in, urging me to confide my sins. After the goose bumps fled, I swayed with trepidation. I felt joy at his safe homecoming and fear that he would turn me in.

Gone was the teasing, that sometimes wicked playfulness visible around the corners of his mouth when he baited me in an attempt to get a reaction. In its place was a bone-weary soldier with bruising along his temple and God only knew where else.

There was nowhere to run. I'd come to him, which meant I was willing to fully wade into the complicated waters of our relationship, whatever that was. An undeniable connection existed between us, one we'd toyed with but backed away from, given its weighty complication.

I turned from his penetrating gaze. I couldn't ignore him, but I needed to escape his magnetic hold, so I walked to the open door that led to the lanai. The cooling trade winds swept inside, stirring my hair and pushing its heaviness from my face. The salty air caressed my skin, loaning me a temporary sense of calm.

"I'm glad you're back. Safe." Wrapping my arms around myself, I kept my back to him. "I had nowhere to go, Ty."

"What's going on, Lina?" he whispered, closer than he had been, his deep voice a heavy caress filled with potential danger.

I needed his help. There would be no tiptoeing around the issues of my presence. "I'm here to figure out what went so terribly wrong." I worried my lip then voiced what had to be out in the open. "You've been back to the base." It wasn't a question, but I waited for him to answer regardless.

"I have." He was closer. I could feel the heat from his body.

The lack of accusation went a long way to bolster my flagging will. "I didn't commit treason. I would never do anything like that." I rubbed a hand over my heart, attempting to ease the phantom ache. It hurt even to utter the words, and I shuddered at what it cost me to say it because there was something else in my past that would be a major problem if it came to light. I told him what I needed to, my next words like a prayer on the wind. "Please let me stay."

Heat surrounded me as Ty closed the remaining distance. When his big hands settled on my shoulders and he pulled me back against him, I relaxed into his chest. I was terrified of the outcome, and the skin-on-skin contact went a long way to offer strength.

All the cards were in his hands. Providing shelter when the government wanted me was harboring a known fugitive, something that would tarnish and condemn his career, his life. All I could do was trust in that strange thread that seemed to keep us coming back to each other, whether it was a knock-down, dragged-out argument about the color of the sky or an inferno of desire we couldn't deny no matter how hard we tried.

He rested his chin on the top of my head, wrapping his arms around me. In the fading light, outlines of palm trees were scattered throughout the landscape in the front and to the sides of his house but not in a way that obstructed the stunning view of darkening water and the fiery ball that dipped below the horizon.

A seabird's cry drew my gaze before it dived and threw its beak beneath the ocean's surface in pursuit of a meal. The surf washed away a flock of birds' footprints while I toyed with the many possibilities for change in my unknown future. Tyler held my immediate fate in his hands, and I trusted him—all teasing, pushing away, and frustrating arguments aside.

"You know the risk of us being here together. What that means for my career."

It was like déjà vu in a sense, and unease swirled in my gut. "I do. But no one knows I'm here. If you keep it that way, the risk is minimized. Please, Ty, I need time to find a mistake by whoever planted information and framed me as the mole." The idea that anyone thought I would allow harm to befall our team was nauseating. "I was thinking of hacking into the database and looking for clues."

"No." He shook his head slowly. "That could make matters worse. I'll come up with another way."

I nodded my agreement, the tension inside me so high that I didn't trust myself to speak. Seconds ticked by while we were locked together, the ocean rolling and shifting before us, heralding the many possible outcomes of his decision. I hoped and prayed we could ride the same wave, that he would help me.

"You can stay."

My body sagged against his, weak with relief. If not for his arms holding me up, I would have fallen to the floor.

"But you'll do things my way in terms of your safety and in who I may choose to involve."

"Okay." I didn't have any arguments for him, as he hadn't said I couldn't help to ferret out the traitor. "Where do we start?" I know I would mentally revisit everything that happened in the office over the last month or so, any odd behavior from our coworkers. It had to have been an inside job. "Someone planted the information." I had my suspicions, but I wasn't sure if he was ready to hear them.

"I'm going to talk with Jack Davis."

I tilted my head so I could read his expression. I'd heard of the former SEALs who occasionally handled sticky rescue-and-recovery situations with the government. Working with them created less red tape for the CIA, and I knew they had deep contacts. "Will it be safe to talk with him, for both of us?"

Ty nodded, his gaze roving over the water before he spun me around so that we were face-to-face. I kept my eyes averted, not wanting him to see how guilty I felt because of my suspicions. He cupped the side of my jaw and caressed my cheek with a thumb, and I leaned into him. I couldn't help it. But his words put all my senses on alert: "You suspect someone."

He knew I was holding back. "I do." But telling him that I thought a friend of his was the traitor was worrisome. I didn't have a choice, not if we were working together to clear my name. "Mark has access to my computer." Because I worked under him, helping him with whatever he needed.

A muscle jumped at the side of his square jaw. "Tell me again what happened. How you got here."

I recounted going to work, Anna meeting me at the door, the brief conversation we'd had in which she relayed that Mark was at my desk with a group of agents, and how she'd told me to go.

"Did you see Mark at your workstation?"

"Anna shifted to the side just enough that I caught a glimpse of him there, surrounded by a handful of agents."

"And you chose to run, rather than dispute whatever was going on?"

My head thunked against his chest. I took measured breaths then mumbled my weak response. "Come on, you know me. That's what I do." *I'm a runner.*

"With us, yes." I shivered as his deep baritone washed over me.

"I couldn't handle the thought of being locked up. I have a bad reaction to it, major claustrophobia. And I don't know. It was the way Anna told me to go. The look in her eyes, it was unsettling." That was only a partial truth. Eventually, I would have to tell him everything.

Ty hooked his finger under my chin, gently prodding me to meet his gaze. "I've known you a long time, Lina. I find it hard to believe you'd run from something other than us. Tell me what else you're hiding. Trust me."

God help me. I did trust him. Tears welled in my eyes, blurring him and creating a protective distance. "There's more. But it doesn't have to do with what's happening now. It's from my past. With my parents." My fingers tightened on his forearms. "I'll tell you. Soon. I need a little more time." I was terrified he would look at me differently, and it wasn't only my life at stake anymore.

His eyes moved restlessly over my face before he gave me a

curt nod. When he released me, I had to lock down my muscles to keep from staggering. I missed the contact instantly. When he ran his fingers through his hair, I let myself take in his unkempt appearance, from the dark shadows under his eyes to the thick growth of hair coating his square jaw.

"When was the last time you slept?" I asked.

He grunted, dropping his bag near the couch then turning toward the bedroom. "Three days ago."

I wrung my hands, feeling like the worst person ever. I hadn't even asked him how he'd gotten home or about the cache of weapons and the hostage. *Is he okay?* "Ty—"

"Let's talk tomorrow." He cut me off as he angled toward the bedroom but turned to look at me over his shoulders, his weary gaze telegraphing profound exhaustion.

I nodded, clutching my iPad to my chest. If he wasn't going to pass out immediately, I had no doubt he needed space. Pivoting on my heel, I went to the lanai and switched on my iPad, swiped to the book I wanted, and settled in to read.

Thirty minutes later, I was on the same sentence. He said he would let me stay, but that could change in the morning. Anxiety over him being home and me not having the place to myself for a few days to work on strategy and possibly uncover clues to prove my innocence sat heavily in my gut. Maybe I should leave before he decided I had to go.

"Lina."

I jumped at his voice. He was so big but moved on silent feet, shadowy and ghostlike, as he must have to be on missions. He took the tablet from me and set it on the small round table at my elbow. With my hand firmly in his, he pulled me to my feet. I followed as he led me to his room. "I said you could stay, and I meant it. But I can hear your mind whirling out there, and I need sleep."

The covers were drawn back, and he ushered me onto the king-sized mattress. When he got behind me, pulling my back to his chest and securing me to him with an arm draped over my waist, I let out a deep sigh. The worry of the day, his haggard appearance, and the possible outcomes faded, and I hoped it would last for the duration of the night. In his arms, I was where I wanted to be. It was something I could admit to myself in the inky darkness that surrounded us. Heat radiated from him and worked like a drug, easing me into sleep in a matter of minutes.

13

MALINA

I awoke to Ty missing from the bed. There was an indentation on his pillow from where his head had rested, but the space next to me was cold. I tamped down on the instant worry over him being gone—he'd probably gone for a run.

After brushing my teeth and eating a few saltines, I went to the lanai to take in another gorgeous day. I'd slept late, and my stomach emitted a continuous grumble that the crackers helped with. It wasn't what I craved, though. I knew what I wanted—coconut milk. I couldn't stop thinking about it.

There were a few brown coconuts on the ground, but I wanted the younger green ones that clung to the palm trees. They were sweeter, and the craving I had wouldn't go away. I could wait for Ty to get back from jogging—maybe he would climb and get them for me. With a few steps, I was at the base of the closest tree, gripping the back of it. Or I could do it.

The balls of my feet pushed against the bark to walk up it as my arms simultaneously pulled. With practiced ease, I scaled the tree then angled myself with my knees on either side of the trunk, squeezing and holding me in place so that I could knock the green coconuts down. I'd loosened two when movement caught my attention.

"Hey, island girl." Ty jogged from the shore toward me. The sunlight glistened off his perspiring body, highlighting how perfectly sculpted he was. A jolt of desire hit me. I remembered running my hands over his corded muscles, feeling all that power beneath my fingertips. Wrapped in his arms the night before had been decadent, but the one we'd spent together not too long ago continued to smolder in my mind.

"Hi." I smiled at him, forcing the image of kissing him in Vegas to stop. I managed to knock down another coconut then repositioned myself to climb down. It appeared that we were ignoring the heavy issues at hand, and I was good with that. I needed a breather from all the stress anyway. "How was your run?"

"Good." He sounded better.

Maybe he would talk to me about what happened when he was captured with the other American, as we'd all assumed. It had to have been awful, and I worried he would have PTSD after the ordeal. So far, he hadn't shown any signs.

As I neared the base of the palm tree, Ty's hands wrapped around my waist, and he lifted me the rest of the way down until my feet were firmly on the ground. "You could have waited. I would have gotten those for you."

I shrugged, stepping away from him, and his hands fell away. I missed the connection instantly, but that was a dangerous game to play. We'd had only two nights together. There was a pattern. My being on his island didn't mean anything would change.

I'd tied my hair on top of my head so that it wouldn't get in the way of climbing the tree. It was already heating up outside, the sand going from cool beneath my toes to warm. I had plans that day that had nothing to do with my predicament. My parents were away and safe, I was hidden, and there was a beach lounger with my name on it, so long as I could get Ty to carry it near the shore for me.

I bent to pick up one of the coconuts. Ty had the other two. Following him into his house, I let my gaze wander over his strong back. My face heated as he looked over his shoulder.

"Put that one on the counter, and I'll open it for you. Do you want one now?"

I pursed my lips. I really did. "Yep."

A grin curved his face, and I blinked to clear my instant daze. He always affected me so much, and the hormones multiplied it by about a billion. I needed to put some space between us for sure.

He used a tapper with ease then screwed in caps for two of them and a straw for the last one. I scooped up the coconuts, put the two with stoppers in a bag with a towel and book, then met his gaze. "Would you mind bringing one of the deck loungers to the beach for me? I tried, but I couldn't get it to fold up, and then there are the cushions." My cheeks heated even more. I should have been able to figure that out, but my patience had worn too thin too quickly. And it was heavy. I wasn't sure how much I should lift while I was pregnant.

"Sure. Give me a sec." He grabbed a glass and filled it with water. "I'll meet you on the beach."

I didn't need him to tell me twice. I said a quick thanks and got the heck out of there. I didn't need to add to my stalkerish ways by staring at him with longing as his throat moved from drinking water. It was such a weird feeling—I was usually able to control my reactions so much better. The last thing I wanted him to know was how much I was into him, especially when I didn't think he liked me all that much, aside from the two one-night stands. I was a challenge for him and probably the only reason why he kept asking me out.

I wanted to call Beth or Anna so badly, but it was too dangerous. Anna wasn't a possibility. She could get in trouble for warning me to run, and I wouldn't contact her and put her at risk just because I was scared and lonely. I couldn't reach out to Beth for many reasons, especially because Mark may have remembered who my friend from high school was and passed that information on to the team investigating my whereabouts.

It was fine. I could keep my own counsel for now.

The sand was soft and warm beneath my bare feet, and the sun climbed higher in the sky, promising a beautiful, cloudless day. The rhythmic back-and-forth of the waves was my favorite sound, and I let all the worries that plagued me fade against the beauty around me.

I peeled off my stretchy T-shirt and shimmied out of my shorts, revealing my dark-red bikini just as Ty set the lounge chair next to me. Guilt slammed into me, and I defended the time I was selfishly doing nothing. "I want to spend a few hours in the sun. Then I'll get some work done." I worried my bottom lip because there was nothing else I could do. Well, there was one thing. I needed to talk to Ty about the familiar man I'd seen at the marina the morning I fled.

Hypnotizing brown eyes met mine, and I froze, waiting for what he would do or say next. "You don't need to make excuses for wanting to relax in the sun. I have some phone calls to make, and then I'll come join you." He waited for a beat, and I sucked in a much-needed breath. "We can talk about what's on your mind then."

Am I that transparent? I nodded then sank onto the lounger as he made his way back to the house. Kicking my feet up on the cushions, I stretched out. As the sun heated my skin and the waves lulled me into a drowsy state, I accepted the truth that I wanted more with him, something real, and that I also needed his help. I wasn't ready to tell him everything. It was ridiculous to leave any piece of information out. But I could let him know about the man I'd spotted on the docks when I'd left Honolulu without revealing the secret I hadn't planned to share with anyone, ever.

I downed the sweet coconut milk, which satisfied my raging thirst. The other two waited, but the sun heating my skin made me drowsy... or the process of growing a baby did. I was tired all the time. At least I'd found out why.

Drifting in and out of sleep, I was vaguely aware of Ty joining me, and even when I heard him talking on the phone, I couldn't bring myself to wake fully. Then he lifted me from the chair and carried me inside with the explanation that I was getting red and needed to get out of the sun for a while.

Once in the house, I stirred awake but didn't protest him cradling me to his chest, as I was content in his arms. When we were at the kitchen table, he released my legs, and they slid down his body. A shiver followed in the wake of the innocent caress, and all fogginess from my nap fled.

When he pulled a chair out and nudged me to sit, a sense of worry invaded my happy bubble. It was time to lay it all out on the table. He slapped a deck of cards on the wooden surface, and I met his gaze over my shoulder with a serenity I didn't feel.

Even if my life depended on it, I could never read Ty's face when he played cards.

"Let's play a game," he murmured behind me, nuzzling my ear. My eyes drifted shut as my desire for him flared to life. We'd hidden behind sarcasm for a year, probably because neither of us knew what to do with the intensity of what was between us—the unchartered waters I wasn't sure I could brave or where they would lead. "We'll play for truths."

He lifted both the chair and me as he scooted me in. I couldn't have helped if I wanted to. The power he had over my body was disturbing.

Answers. He'd meant answers about what had happened at work, why I'd run—the real reason. There were secrets that would be detrimental to my staying in the States, and I didn't want to share. But I wasn't guilty of treason, and that was what he wanted—needed—to find out.

By the time he'd found some poker chips, I'd regained enough control to be able to look him in the eyes without giving away the fact that I was scared and on the verge of falling into his arms all over again. I had zero willpower where he was concerned.

We played in silence, using only the chips as ante to the pot. But I knew that wouldn't last. There were things that needed to be said between us, and we were good at avoiding hard truths. I knew the game was his way of drawing me out and maybe sharing a few things of his own in the process. When that happened, secrets would be the currency.

The mound of chips grew between us, neither having much left to add to the ante. I was close to laying my cards on the table when a mischievous glint flickered in Ty's eyes. It was the same look he'd gotten when he'd gone up against an opponent in high school. There were very few ways that he telegraphed his moves, but he'd just allowed one to shine through. If he hadn't wanted me to see it, I never would have. My teeth sunk into my bottom lip. *What is up his sleeve?*

When he dug into his jeans pocket, I sat up straight. *Are we making things personal with the pot? What is he going to throw into the pile?* I held my breath, shocked at the square-cut diamond ring he set on top of the chips with care. The light reflected the fire within the stone, and my head swam. There was something very familiar about it. "Is that your mom's?"

He replied with a slow shake of his head.

Anxiety built in the pit of my stomach as bits and pieces of the night in Vegas danced through my mind. There were words spoken, the weight of the ring, and then a kiss. Dizziness threatened to overwhelm me. "Did we?"

A grin spread across his mouth. "We did, Malina Hale."

Another name. On the heels of his words came the truth of

what I had to share. If we were dropping bombs on each other, I had one too. My purse was within reach. I went to it and dug around inside until I found what I wanted. When I returned to my seat, I met his penetrating stare, firming my resolve. "I'll see your ante." I placed the positive pregnancy stick next to the ring. "And raise it."

When he tore his gaze from mine to land on the two pink lines on the test-strip window, it was as if all the air was sucked out of the room. An unnatural stillness came over him, and I felt like prey in its wake. I didn't dare move. Then he lifted his eyes to mine. The emotions swirling in his made me sway with the weight of them and the promise they held. "You're pregnant? With our child?"

I nodded. "I guess we didn't use any protection." I remembered only snippets of the night we'd shared in Vegas, the rest lost in a haze of intoxication.

"We did, but nothing is foolproof." He stood, never breaking eye contact. Once next to me, he took my hand in his, urging me to stand before him. My heart thumped against my chest in a loud, percussive beat. No words were said, but thousands were exchanged in the promise in his eyes. He bent, closing the distance between us, his hands falling to my hips and mine onto his shoulders.

His forehead rested against mine, and our breath mingled. Heat infused me from his touch, and tingles danced along my exposed skin at his nearness. We stood on another precipice, one where we would make a life-altering choice, and I was ready for it.

"The ring changed things between us. The words we spoke that night bound us on one level. The baby"—he said the word with reverence, and my knees buckled, supported by his strength—"ties us together for life. I want this, Lina. Do you?"

"I do." And I meant it. In secret, I'd crushed on Ty ever since Beth dated him and we swore off the Hale men forever. At the time, I'd needed a friend more than a boyfriend, despite the way he'd made me feel. Now, I wanted both a best friend and a lover, which Ty and I would be for each other.

His hand shifted, dipped beneath my T-shirt, and splayed over my stomach. "How are you feeling?"

I melted. The guy was so large and tough, but the way he handled me was incredibly gentle. "I'm good. Just a little queasy at times."

"No more games. No more running, Lina."

My back straightened. "I'm not the one who played games." I started ticking off movie titles. "*How to Lose a Guy in 10 Days, Runaway Bride—*"

"The movies were about wanting to spend time with you." Straight white teeth flashed as his grin stretched wide. "And I only chose those titles to get a rise out of you, to try to get you to lighten up and go out with me again." He shrugged. "And maybe as a subtle hint with that last one."

"I didn't even know we were married!" I smacked his shoulder.

His smile fell away, and his expression turned serious. "I should have told you that morning, but you had your deer-in-headlights thing going on and had one foot out the door as soon as you woke up."

"I know." I would have to change my ways. I couldn't run from what-if situations. I had to stop putting my heartbreak and fear over what had happened to Samuel on him. "I want this."

He drew me tightly into his embrace, and I let go of all my fears, at least for the time being. After all, it wasn't very often that I found out I was married and told my new husband we were having a child in one day.

MALINA

"Let's go for a walk." He eased my iPad from my grip then linked our hands and drew me outside. We didn't speak as we made our way to the shore. I wanted to talk with Ty about what he'd learned from his contacts. The militia soldier at the marina continued to worry me, especially if he was there to finish what he'd started before. Rubbing up against the past, the uncertainty of our future had stolen the heat from my body, and the void filled with fear.

I attempted to push the concern from my thoughts, focusing on the soft sand between my toes and how natural it was to walk side by side with that man. The sun warmed my shoulders, and I hadn't realized how much I needed it. But being hand in hand with Ty and watching the frothy surf rushing to meet our feet only to retreat before the cycle started again eased the anxiety that was building in me. There were questions for which I wanted answers. "Would you take back what happened in Vegas? The marriage, the baby?"

He stopped and turned me to him, his large hands gripping my shoulders. "I wouldn't change a second of that night. If we had been sober and I thought I could get away with it, I still would have proposed right then and there. I've wanted you for a long time, Lina. It's you that pushed me away."

"Beth—"

"Wasn't you. I dated her, but I was never that into her. I thought you knew that."

In a way, I had. But there were doubts. So many. He'd always been on the top tier in high school. Girls clamored for any attention from him. But I'd guarded my grief-stricken heart.

"The first time I saw you was the last day I went out with Beth, and it was like a punch to the gut. You stole all the air in my lungs. But you were so haunted, and I knew that look because of how Kayla was after losing her brother. I wasn't ready for you then. I knew it. That's also why I didn't pursue you. There was something about you that screamed 'long-term commitment.' I always hoped we'd get together. Then when we did last year—"

"And I ran." I grinned. I couldn't help it. "You're a lot to take in. That night." I sighed because it was a memory I'd replayed over and over since it'd happened. Ty wasn't someone I could ever forget. No one would compare what he did to me, how he made me feel, and how I reacted to his touch. "I was afraid." I'd instinctively known he was the one person who could destroy me, especially if I let myself fall and love him more than I thought he could ever care for me. A year before, I'd lost a part of my heart to him that I knew I would never get back. It would always be his.

He flashed me a crooked grin. "You ran, and I took offense."

I laughed. He had. "There were so many verbal wars that week. I was almost relieved when you had to go on a mission. It was a reprieve to regroup."

"I haven't gone out with anyone else since then."

"For a year?" I couldn't have kept the surprise from my tone even if I'd tried. I hadn't dated, but for him, that was not at all how I pictured him, based on his high school prowess.

"You got under my skin, and I liked it. I couldn't figure out how to change your opinion of me. Of us."

That was on me. "Because I wouldn't let you."

He nodded.

"But marriage. Were you aware of what was going on? You drank as much as I did."

He dropped his forehead to mine, his long lashes dropping as he closed his eyes. "I was so into you—am into you. Something came over me, and I kept thinking of you like a Koa butterfly. So stunning and elusive, fluttering in and out of my life. I wanted to capture you so you couldn't leave me again. It wasn't the right way to think of a relationship. I couldn't trap you in a jar and keep you for myself, even though I wanted to. You were the girl that got away. I'm not going to make that same mistake again."

"I..." My mind deserted me. What he said was beautiful, minus the capture-in-a-jar part, and I didn't know how to respond.

"Then I asked you to marry me. We were dancing, and joy radiated from you like the sun breaking through the clouds. Intoxicating. The words were out of my mouth, and I didn't want to take them back. I asked, and you said yes."

I tiled my head because a part of me didn't believe it. "You asked me? You got down on one knee?"

He straightened, our foreheads no longer touching. The intimate moment lessened. "No. I was drunk too. I think I said something like, 'let's get married.' And you said 'sure.'"

Huh, that made sense. "I don't remember the ceremony. Or even waking with the ring on my finger."

He rubbed the back of his neck, and my temper stirred.

"You didn't say anything in the morning. Are you sure you don't regret it?"

"Not even a little. But you weren't ready to hear what had happened. Especially with how you left."

That sexy grin pulled his lips up, and I had to fight the way my heart fluttered in response, holding tightly to my irritation. "We can just get the marriage annulled if that was your plan."

"A little late for that, don't you think?" He tugged on a handful of my hair that the wind had pushed over my shoulder to dance along his bare chest. "Even if I wanted an annulment, which I don't"—his palm pressed against my still-flat stomach —"it isn't possible."

I crossed my arms over my chest. I just couldn't let it go. He should have confessed in the morning and stopped me from leaving. "But you entertained the idea of it when you woke up?"

He grabbed my hands so that I wouldn't whirl around and storm off. I was close to doing it, and he held me in place to talk.

"I removed the rings from our fingers because I wanted to talk to you about what we did and break the news to you gently. Especially after the crazy sex we had that night. I wanted a repeat when I woke up, not to have you mad at me."

Please. That wasn't easy to believe. I rolled my eyes so hard I almost fell over. "So it's really about the sex." It was incredible but not what a marriage should be based on. I tugged to break free and storm off, needing to think and cool down. The mercurial pregnancy hormones were so not helping me.

But he wasn't having it. "Look at me, Lina. It was crazy hot between us because of how I feel about you. I've wanted you for years. This is our time now. We're both mature enough... I mean, it took me long enough."

Against my will, I softened. *Why does he have to be so... everything?* "Okay, I understand your thought process about not telling me right away. I didn't make it easy for you that morning." *Confession time.* "I was mad at myself. Not you. I felt vulnerable."

His broad shoulders eclipsed my view and blocked the glare from the water. Hormones raged through my body, and I was dangerously close to tears with how sweet he was.

"We have a mountain of an obstacle in our way, but I promise you, we will overcome it together."

I managed a nod before the dam broke, and my eyes filled with tears that my eyelashes failed to contain. Ty gathered me in his arms, and I realized something that I'd fought when he'd held me in the past. In his embrace, I was home.

After I got control of myself, I stepped back, needing some space so we could talk about what to do about that obstacle. "What are we going to do?" I didn't want him to handle my predicament in his take-charge manner. It was my fight too.

He ran his fingers through his hair, mussing the dark strands into a sexy bedhead look. "We're going to have to draw Mark out and orchestrate the situation so he makes a mistake."

I opened my mouth to say what I knew was the best way to do that, but he stopped me.

"No. You're not going to be bait."

"I didn't even say anything." I curled my fists and set them at my hips, elbows thrust out. He could be so frustrating at times.

His hands found my waist and tugged me forward, my arms transferring from my hips to lay flat on his chest. "We'll find another way, Island Girl. I can't risk anything happening to you."

My heart melted. He had that effect.

"Give me a chance to talk things over with my contact at the Gray Ghost team, and I'd like to run options by my brothers too."

I dug my teeth into the side of my lower lip, contemplating everything he said. We were on the same team, married, and having a baby together. I had to trust that we would come up with a plan, that everything would work out, and that he was the best man to help me. I nodded. When his arms enveloped me back into their steely strength, I let him shoulder some of the pressure. I was relieved.

15

— — —

MALINA

Blanketed in darkness, I toed the edge of the surf, digging my feet in the sand. The salty air swept my heavy hair away from my neck and back like a rippling flag dancing in the wind. Stars peppered the sky, and a crescent moon hung low, offering a sliver of silvery light across the choppy water. In the dreamscape, I could tiptoe along its path and into the arms of the gods but not in reality. I was awake, the emptiness inside growing into a vast, cavernous hole as the wind picked up and dark clouds rolled in the distance.

What am I doing? I wanted Ty but not to the point of risking his future too. The longer I stayed in the wind, on the run, the greater the damage would be to both of us. My hand splayed across my belly, and I squared my shoulders. I wasn't looking out just for myself anymore. Things would change, and I needed to secure a safe future. Ty had a team working on it, but I had to pull my own weight and trace the trail from the past couple of months. The problem was, it inevitably led back to Mark. I'd already told Ty I suspected him, but it was time to talk about entrapping his friend. Even though he didn't want me to come out of hiding, the best way to lure

Mark and any accomplices into the open was if they went after me.

Strong arms wound around me and pulled me against a hard chest. I hadn't heard Ty's approach, and a jolt of adrenaline shot through me. But that was to be expected—he moved on silent feet. He'd been trained to be smoke, the elusive shadow in the night, to strike before the enemy sensed his presence. It was ingrained in him.

"What's going on in that pretty head of yours?" He nuzzled my neck, contorting his large body around mine, chasing away the chill of the approaching storm. "Counting stars or planning world denomination?"

"World domination. Always." I couldn't help but smile and relax, fitting myself into him as if it was the most natural thing to do. The wind whipped my hair into a messy tornado as the storm raced to greet us, obscuring the night sky as the clouds moved in more quickly. The weather was as mercurial as my moods. "Why are you awake?"

"Mmm, I sensed a disturbance in the force." He pressed a kiss to my neck.

Banked desire roared to life at his gentle touch. I tilted my head to allow him greater access. He didn't disappoint and trailed his lips to the crook of my neck, where he nipped, and I sucked in a breath, the flame growing into an inferno. Need and want took me hostage, all thoughts of my predicament reduced to ash at our feet.

I found my wildest fantasies in his arms. I shivered as the air turned chilly, and the first drops of rain splashed across the turbulent waves and upon our heads. Lightning split the sky. Electricity charged the air. It only added to the passion between us. Ty's arms swept under my legs, and he lifted me to cradle against his chest. Thunder crackled then exploded in a deafening boom, raising all the fine hairs along my body.

He bent his head, his lips teasing my nape. I arched my neck to give him greater access, shivering as he whispered words against my skin.

"You, baby girl, have always been the one that got away. I've wanted more from you than you were willing to give."

"Seems you've got me now."

"I do, my runaway bride."

I couldn't help but grin.

"Let's go inside." His deep voice rumbled in a sensual caress where our skin was pressed together, and a wave of desire replaced the levity of his words. He was right—he did have me. I toyed with my lower lip between my teeth at the thrill of my own personal white knight saving me from being struck by lightning. It was going to be a raging storm, both inside the house and out.

Whether I wanted one or not, I needed a hero. And in Ty, I would always have one.

The patio door shut behind us as the sky opened into a deluge of rain. He didn't release me until we reached his bedroom. My legs slid down his body. He'd come to me in black boxer briefs that clung to his body, leaving nothing to the imagination. I felt the hard press of him against me and shivered in anticipation.

One of his large hands remained at my hip, tethering me to him, while the other cupped my cheek. I felt the edge of the proverbial cliff we both stood on. The final moments before a life-altering decision would be made were something I was intimately familiar with.

Strobing light flashed in the room as lightning crisscrossed the night sky, highlighting the desire that morphed Ty's handsome features from stunning to breathtaking. I melted on the spot at the heat reflected in his dark eyes. His fingers trailed the curve of my cheek. "I want you, Lina, for more than tonight. When I said my vows to you, regardless of the circumstances that brought them about or the condition we were in, it's what I wanted. I meant every word, every promise. You're the one I want to share my life with. But you have a choice. You're not trapped. I'll help you no matter what you decide."

Again, he reassured me. Everything in me stilled at the leashed power of the man who held me. He tensely waited for my response.

I felt myself sinking into his capable embrace as he shielded me from the wind and rain bracketing the side of the house. "That's a loaded couple of statements there." The man would topple anything in his way to protect what he considered his. It was time to drop my barriers. I would commit physically and mentally. "I choose you." Even whisper soft, the words echoed inside my head and heart, binding me to him in ways even I didn't understand.

"All right, baby girl. There's no going back now. Know that your fights are my fights."

I melted. Ty was a force. Having all that power at my fingertips was a heady thing indeed. His lips brushed across mine, and all thought fled. Tingles danced over my skin in the wake of his touch, and I pressed closer. My mouth parted on a sigh. He swallowed the sound and swept his tongue inside. I let myself mold fully against his body, and we fit together as if we were made to.

Then he lifted me, and my legs wrapped around him.

When he drew back to readjust our position, I clung to him. I let the desire flame to its fullest then lifted my eyes to his, baring my soul. It was time to let go of the walls around my heart because the man was worth everything. His eyes dilated, and he drew me close, angling his head toward mine. At the touch of his lips, my eyelids fluttered closed. Our tongues met in a teasing dance until I arched against him, needing to be closer, wanting to crawl into his skin.

His fingers threaded through my hair, cradling my head as he deepened the kiss. Somehow, we had reached the bed, and he lowered me onto the mattress. I whimpered until he followed, welcoming the weight of his body pressing into mine. I trailed my fingers up his arm and shoulder to sink into his thick hair, desperate for more.

A gasp left me as he tore his mouth from mine only to trail kisses from the corner of my mouth, along my jawline, and finally to my neck. My skin heated, and I suddenly became aware of the offensive barrier of our clothes. I tugged at his shirt until he eased back and pulled it over his head. Then he helped me. In record time, our clothes lay wherever we'd thrown them. I shivered as I felt him against my core.

A spike of desire shot through me, and I ground my hips against his hard length. His mouth and fingers teased me, and I moaned. When lightning flashed, filling the room with its strobe effect, I sucked in a breath at the sight of the godlike man before me. I hungrily ate up everything about him, his lips swollen from our kisses, the harsh desire that pulled his chiseled features taut. The muscles in his arms flexed and bulged as he held himself up so that he didn't crush me.

He chuckled, but I couldn't tear myself away from the feast to figure out why. My fingers roamed over his sinfully sexy six-pack while I plotted everything I wanted to do to him. When his fingers nudged my chin up so that I looked at him, I could only stare in confusion. My brain was hazy with passion and need. It took that mischievous grin of his to infuse a semblance of sanity. "What?"

"Are you sure?"

My brows furrowed, and a spike of irritation infused my blood. I huffed out a breath. "You aren't seriously asking me that, are you? Yes, I'm more than sure. And before you say it, I won't run in the morning."

His laugh caused a ripple of flexing muscles, and I no longer cared why he thought that was funny. Lust built inside me, making me more than ready for him, and I lifted my hips, seeking that delicious friction.

When his hand curled around my hip, another jolt of desire flooded me. He teased my entrance, and we both moaned as he entered then filled me, slowly and sensually at first but turning hard and fast. I pushed against him, needing something more. He changed the angle, and my world spun out of control. Growling, he increased the pace, bringing me higher until stars burst behind my eyelids. With a deep thrust, he followed, chasing me as I fell apart in his arms.

I gasped for air. He dropped his head to the crook of my neck, and we stayed like that until our racing hearts slowed to a manageable tempo.

When he pulled out, I whimpered at the loss. He shifted to his side then pulled me against him. As I lay in his arms, the storm raged outside. Neither of us said anything. The patter of rain against the windows and the crashing waves just beyond the swaying palm trees lulled us into a sense of contentment. My last thought before I succumbed to sleep in his embrace was that for the first time in a very long time, I felt complete.

16

MALINA

My usual morning ritual of rushing to the bathroom and hurling was postponed. Ty had set crackers and water on the nightstand on my side of the bed before we went to sleep. His thoughtfulness scored points, but there were so many what-ifs swimming around in my head. I'd ended up slipping from the bed then grabbing a T-shirt, my cardigan, and a pair of panties to go see how the storm had rearranged the shore.

A chill lingered in the air from the cool night before, and the trade winds blew across the island and rustled palm fronds, the sound mingling with the rolling waves. I shivered as my bare feet met the cool white sand. The sun inched above the horizon but not high enough to chase away the remnants of the post-storm effects.

Shells dotted the shore. I found a relatively seaweed-free place to sit, pulled my knees to my chest, and wrapped my arms around them. With my chin resting on my bent legs, I gazed out at the ever-changing ocean, contemplating what life with Ty and a new baby would be like. *Would we even have a chance at one?*

My heels dug into the sand. There was so much against us,

keeping us at a distance, regardless of his words last night or of how physically attracted we were to each other.

I felt his warmth at my back as he joined me in the sand, never hearing his approach, and gave in as he pulled me to lean against him. His legs bracketed mine. Cocooned by his body, I gazed at the vast expanse of blue and frothing waves.

"Did you have trouble sleeping?" He gathered my hair, twisted it twice, and lay the heavy mass over my left shoulder.

"No. I slept great, and the crackers took care of my temperamental stomach. Thanks for that."

"Mmm-hmm." A few seconds passed while his fingers idly rubbed along my sweater-clad arms. "Then what pulled you from bed so early?"

It was time I let him glimpse my crazy a little more. "What kind of future do we really have, Ty? I mean, this is fantastic while we're living in a bubble of our own making. But that'll change. Your brothers will come here, and the government will find me, and I can't have all of you affected by harboring a suspect wanted for treason."

"We discussed this last night when I told you that your battles are also mine. Buckle up. I'm not letting you go. We'll find out who the guilty party is and clear you of any accusations."

"Let's say that, by some miracle, all charges are dropped. You and I, how is that going to work? We're getting along now, but on a normal day, we're fighting."

His fingers found the ends of my hair and played with it, twisting the strands around his finger and releasing it only to do it all over again. It was soothing and distracting at the same time.

"Let's talk about the past. You like to come back to how I briefly dated your friend Beth. But there are things you don't know about that time. And how when I saw you that first time our senior year, I didn't stand a chance. You were grieving. That much I could see, but I didn't know details of why you were so haunted. When I went anywhere near you, impenetrable walls went up, and later, you chose to run away from anything to do with me. I knew you were protecting yourself."

He wasn't wrong. "You went through girls like water. And Beth, she was my only real friend. I wasn't ready for you then. Even now, I'm still scared."

"You don't need to be afraid with me. I'm here to stay. And the fighting… anytime I get too close, your natural instincts take over, and you use bickering to hold me back. I'm not innocent in that. It's fun to spar with you, and I tend to egg you on." He flashed me one of his heart-stopping grins. "Because I think you hide behind my dating one of your friends back in high school as an excuse. Let's talk about Beth and put those barriers to rest."

Heat stained my cheeks, but I played along despite how accurate his assessment was. "She's happily married with a couple of kids. We talk on occasion. What did you want to know?"

"Good for her. That's not what I meant, though."

I tried another tactic. "She was devastated when you went out with Annabelle, then Jill, and the list goes on. You broke her heart."

"How so? I never asked her to be my girlfriend. There were no promises made. She knew what she was getting into when we went out a few times."

Even I had known that she shouldn't have read into them casually dating. She'd told me that neither of them had uttered words of commitment, and he'd made it clear they weren't dating. It was all in her head. But he was the unicorn, the one so many of us wanted. Well, not me. I recognized how desirable he was; I just hadn't allowed myself to act on it. Not for a long time. I couldn't—the boy who held all my firsts and I'd thought my lasts had died the night I'd left Venezuela. It wasn't something I could snap back from. I'd needed time. So much of it. "I don't want my heart to be broken like hers was." I didn't have much of it left to begin with. It was buried with Samuel and my parents. "I know we were teenagers, but that doesn't change the fear I have about what it'll be like when you leave."

"I wasn't ready to have a long-term girlfriend back then. I knew I was enlisting and would go on deployments. It wasn't the right time, although when I met you, something just clicked. I'd never experienced it before. I sensed that you were the one I shouldn't let get away, and that things would be different between us."

"And now is the right time?"

"Yes." His thumb brushed the curve of my bottom lip. "But that's not really what this is all about, is it?" His fingers touched under my chin, and he tilted my head so that our gazes met, my body shifting to the side but supported by his other arm. "The past is an excuse, one I don't think you're all that hung up on anymore. There's something else holding you back, and I hope you'll share that with me soon. I get that the main concern we need to deal with is what's going on with work, with the risk to our future. But I want to know all of you, even the things you think aren't important. Everything about you is."

Damn it. When I thought about it, that hit home, not the stuff about our past. "The defensiveness is ingrained from the pact Beth and I made." *And because of my need to protect my heart.* I was embarrassed to say it, but we were being honest. "I needed her at that time in my life. It seemed fair to agree not to date you. Girl code and all. I think I felt a little guilty when we went out a year ago… and what it led to." I rested my head against his arm. "I did tell her."

"Stop hiding from me. You're different, always have been."

I couldn't stop the twisted thoughts from finding a voice. He had to know, at some point anyway. "There are things you don't know about my family. You never met my cousin, but we shared so many similar traits."

"I don't need to. I want you. I've always been into you."

I could have told him my cousin was crazy, but given what he'd said, it wouldn't have mattered. He was invested in me, no matter what. My heart fluttered at his words, and another piece of the wall I'd erected toppled to the ground. "We're doing this, then?"

"We are." He grinned again, and I was lost.

———

THE MIDDAY SUN sparkled off the azure waters, and I let the screen door slam behind me. I couldn't be inside any longer. Ty was on the phone with either his brothers or the Gray Ghost team, who had connections that he thought could help us figure out the mess I was in. Being excluded from the conversation made me agitated, but I also didn't want to deal with it. My mood was all over the place.

That was why I found myself outside on the beach. I liked that Ty and I were the only ones on the island—I needed the isolation, but that would change when his brothers arrived. Despite what he'd said, I didn't think I should stay. My presence was putting them all in danger.

Ty appeared beside me, and I jumped about a foot then turned to him, a scowl already in place. "Don't do that! Make some noise when you're sneaking up on me."

He chuckled. "What's going on in that head of yours?"

I huffed out a breath. I needed to relax and learn to expect him to appear the way he did. It was his job to be stealthy. We did need to talk, though, which was one of the reasons I was so on edge. "I'm frustrated because there's nothing I can do. I can't hack into my workstation to see if there are any clues about who planted whatever it was there that labeled me as a traitor. And I'm worried about who it is." I had reached the tricky part.

"Spill it. Why are you worried?" He linked our hands and tugged me so that we were walking along the shore together. Frothy waves broke at our feet, offering relief from the heat of the sun and the humidity clinging to the air.

"Well, because Mark is your friend."

"You don't need to worry about that. I can't ignore it if there's a chance that he's responsible for the leaked intel and the death of my teammates. I have suspicions about him as well. We're looking into it."

I pulled his hand so he stopped and faced me. "And you didn't think to share that with me? Any information affects me. Don't keep me in the dark."

He studied me for several seconds before giving me a solemn nod. "Going forward, I won't."

"Good. Now, tell me everything."

"As Mark has access to your computer, it made sense for us to look into him. Then there's the possible connection of Kyle's death. It's a reach, but those two hated each other."

"Enough for Mark to have him targeted and killed on Xander's last mission?"

"I'll admit that it's a stretch. But it may have been known by his contact and considered a favor. I can't leave or overlook any possibility." He shrugged a well-defined shoulder, and the ripple of muscle momentarily distracted me. "It's a place to start, and friends of ours are digging deep to see if there's a connection."

"Okay." That was better. I could live with that type of information even if I didn't have all the details. But I couldn't help but worry about the baby, our future, and my place supporting the SEAL team. There were changes I wanted to make if I was cleared of all the charges. And I wanted to tell him about those, as we were supposed to be a team. I linked our fingers. "I enjoyed serving our country in the small way I was. I was proud to do so. But now, after all this, I don't want to go back." Even saying it was a huge weight off my shoulders.

"Then don't."

The easy acceptance in his voice filled me with warmth, and I relaxed the death grip I had on his hand.

He gave me a gentle tug, and we resumed our walk along the shore.

"Stay here, on the island. I only have another year until I decide if I want to re-up or not. If I don't, I can always work on an as-needed basis with the Gray Ghost team like my brothers are doing."

"I don't see how I could remain here. I need to get a job, especially since I'll have to support a child."

Ty tugged on my hand to stop me then turned us to face one another. His hands settled on my hips, linking us. "What are you talking about? I'm in this with you. We're together, and nothing is going to change that. The baby is ours to raise, and you don't have to work. I have more than enough money to support you and our children."

"I don't feel married," I whispered past trembling lips, the words hanging between us like a dark cloud. "You remember that night. I don't. The memories are fragmented, and it doesn't feel real to me."

He cupped my cheek, his eyes full of emotion. I leaned into his touch, and that familiar jolt of heat followed. When his hand settled back on my hip, I was dizzy with want. But I needed to know I was worth him asking for my hand when we were fully present and not while intoxicated.

"Let's change that when my brothers are here." The air around us shifted, his broad shoulders eclipsing the world from my view so all that existed was him. "We'll renew our vows. You're the one I want to spend the rest of my life with. Stay here with me. Let's make the island a home for our children and us. Will you be my wife, Malina?"

Tears filled my eyes, and I swallowed the lump in my throat. "Yes." It was all I could manage. Even with the threat hanging over my head, that incredible man wanted to commit his life to mine. My fingers trailed over his chiseled features, careful of the healing bruises from his last mission. He'd never been more handsome, which was saying a lot because he was everything I'd ever wanted.

17

MALINA

Ty and I sat in chairs around a bonfire on the beach. The ocean was calm, and the breeze gently ruffled the fronds not far from where we were. Flames danced against the inky night, embers cracking and sparking in a soothing hiss as they climbed the sky and reached for the stars. My mind was foggy from the two-hour coma-like nap I'd fallen into after dinner. The pregnancy wasn't all that bad, so long as I had crackers and water before even setting foot on the floor in the mornings.

Ty added another log to the bonfire before dropping into a chair next to me. "Tell me something about your family." He pressed a cool drink in my hand from the small table he had set up next to his chair earlier. "It's coconut water."

I took a tentative sip. His deep voice drew me further from my groggy state, and my mind swam with heaviness with what I needed to tell him. I had to remind myself that he was helping me. Not only that, but if we were to have any kind of life together, I owed him the truth.

He moved the logs around with two long sticks, and the flames roared higher, embers crackling and dancing only to fade to black against the sky. The fire bathed us in enough light to see one another.

Silence stretched between us as he waited for me to answer him. It was time I let him in. There was no turning back. "My mom was a twin."

"Was?" He stilled, his perceptive gaze finding mine.

"Yeah, I'll come back to that." I cleared my throat, recentering. "She and her sister were identical in looks but polar opposites in personalities. Two of those differences were their choice in husbands and where they wanted to live. My aunt took after my grandmother. Ambition was ingrained in her, and she studied abroad to be a doctor. A pediatrician. When she fell in love and married an American lawyer, she remained with him in Darien, Connecticut. They had a son and daughter."

"Are they nearby?" Ty shifted next to me and entwined our fingers, his palm warm against my suddenly cold and clammy one.

I nodded, keeping my gaze focused on the flames because I was afraid to see the condemnation that would taint his features once he heard the end of my story. "They live close." I wasn't at that point yet. I wanted him to understand a little about the differences between my mom and my aunt first. "Back to my parents. Madre didn't have the same drive in the sense of wanting a career for herself, but she did when it came to marriage." My fingers tightened on his.

He let the silence settle between us until I was ready to continue.

It was hard to talk about them and reveal something I hadn't shared with anyone. "The match she found for herself was a good one, and mi padre rose in his political career to the inner circle of the president." I fell silent again, considering what else I needed to say. I had to clarify soon, because it wasn't the president Ty would probably have thought I meant. He knew next to nothing about my family. No one did. Except

Beth. She was the only friend I had taken home and who had met my parents. But even she didn't know the details surrounding my home life.

"I'm jumping all over the place, but I want to tell you about my cousin, so you'll understand the parallel between our families. We looked a lot alike, and other than our names, that's where the similarities ended. Since our moms were twins, and we were born in the same month, they thought it was fitting to use my first name for her middle, and her first for mine. Malina Gabriela and Gabriela Malina. Anyway, she and I didn't get along."

"Is that a twin thing? The similar names?"

"I don't really know. But it was something unusual they did to try to dissolve the distance between them." I had to laugh. It was that or cry. And there had been some good times with my cousin. "My aunt and Madre used to say it was as if we were switched at birth. My cousin was pure drama, as if her blood was infused with it. And she was a little fanatical. Those two combinations got her into a ton of trouble. Her brother and I were the more analytical ones. We were cautious, where she leapt with both feet before looking where she would land. A lot like mi madre, actually.

"The day I arrived on my aunt and uncle's doorstep, they'd just come home from the beach. They looked like hell, and my aunt was clutching a ratty-looking cloth to her chest. They fell all over me, crying and hugging me." A large pop and hiss sounded from the fire, and I jumped.

Ty squeezed my hand, encouraging me to continue without words.

"I didn't understand what was going on at first. But their broken sentences fitted together, along with the wet and bloody shirt, so I got the gist of it. They didn't seem to know it was me —they'd thought Malina had miraculously survived a boating accident, even though my aunt clutched a shredded and bloodstained piece of their daughter's shirt in her hands, evidence of what happened to her in those waters."

"Malina? I don't understand. That's your name."

I suppressed a shudder. "I'm getting there, promise. Grief does strange things to people."

"So they thought you were their daughter?"

"Yes, for a few brief moments." That part was twisted, and I hated putting words to my state of mind at that time. "I was okay with it. Especially after what had happened." I pushed out a breath, gathering strength. "What I'm telling you has been in my family vault for years. It needs to stay between us. And since we're married, I'm asking you to respect that, to create a vault of our own."

He tucked a strand of hair behind my ear. "You know I have your back, or you wouldn't have come here. Just tell me, Lina."

"I was wrapped in my own grief at that time. My cousin was partying on a boat then died when sharks attacked her after she most likely fell overboard. None of the kids survived. They were all drunk, and the blood… well, you get where I'm going with that. Not all the parents knew who had gone out that night. Her death happened while I was on a plane from Venezuela after seeing mis padres die in an explosion."

"I'm sorry, Island Girl. I wish I could have been there for you."

I shifted closer to him in my beach chair. The sentiment was sweet, and I appreciated it, but there was more to tell. "I'll never forget the day I left home. Something was brewing with the president of Venezuela, and my friends and I were in opposition to what was being done to our home, to the people. I knew behind closed doors that mis padres were opposed to the injustice too. What I didn't understand at the time was since they were in his inner circle, they were in danger if they didn't agree with and support his every decision." I gave him a quick summary about what I'd done with Samuel and my friends.

"Knowing they were at risk, they wanted me to leave Venezuela. To be safe. They gave me a mini USB flash drive that was hidden inside mi madre's gold-and-turquois locket necklace. I was to go to my aunt and uncle's house in Connecticut and give my uncle the thumb drive, which held sensitive information about the president of Venezuela. They said it would guarantee my new identity, and they would follow when they could. They'd kissed me goodbye and whisked me to a waiting car to take me to the airport. Not long after the car drove away, the house exploded. I'll never forget how the ground shook or the sound. Their deaths are on my hands."

"Come here." Ty lifted me onto his lap and wrapped his arms around me. "The loss suffered by your family in such a short span of time is terrible. I understand why you keep it close. But the explosion... I'm surprised they weren't shot. That seems significant somehow."

Maybe. I didn't really know. Air wheezed from my lungs as I tried to regain control, but Samuel's handsome face with his kind eyes and shaggy brown hair swam in my memories. "That's not it." I dropped my barriers and shared about Samuel, how much I'd loved him, that he'd gone back to defend me, and that because of me, he, too, was dead.

Ty rocked me back and forth as I sobbed, making a mess of his shirt. "Shh, I've got you."

I let him comfort me, and when I was under enough control, I eased back and launched into the rest of my story. "My aunt and uncle became my parents. I'll always mourn my real ones, but after the closed and very secret adoption, I've only referred to them as 'Mom' and 'Dad.' They've done so much for me. And by giving me their daughter's identity, they saved me."

"Is there a record of their daughter's death?"

I shook my head. "No. Malina Gabriela Johannson died that night, but that's a fact known only by her parents. As far as the rest of the world is concerned, I am her. The explosion that killed my family was also thought to have ended my—I mean Gabi's life."

"That's an incredible story. And I understand why you were so grief-stricken our senior year in high school. But you have to know that you did not kill your parents. The president and his militia did."

"Logically, I know that. But my heart never will."

Ty tugged me close, and we stared into the flames, letting our thoughts settle, just being there for each other. It was exactly what I needed.

When his phone rang, he pulled it from his pocket, glancing at the lit screen. "I'm sorry, give me a sec. It's Xander."

I murmured, "okay" then rested my head against his shoulder, grateful that his brother called when he did. It gave me a moment to regroup after telling Ty what I held so close… until I heard Ty mention my family, Venezuela, and the explosion that had killed them. I bolted from the chair, fury cracking like a whip, radiating from every inch of me, and fueling me to action.

In a flash, I was off his lap and sprinting across the sand to the house. I yanked the door to the lanai open and stomped inside. I could hear Ty behind me and whirled around to snap at him. "I can't believe you."

His hand curled around the door before it could slam, and he prowled after me.

"What part of 'this is in the vault' do you not understand?" I air quoted then crossed my arms over my chest. I was so mad I was shaking. Where I'd come from wasn't something I shared with anyone. I'd trusted him and had obviously made the wrong decision.

"You're overreacting."

I jerked back as if he'd slapped me. "Overreacting?" I cringed at the shrill sound of my voice. "I told you about mis padres, how they died, and how I came to be here illegally." Sort of. "And you think it's okay to talk to your brother about any of those details? As if I'm not in enough trouble already?" I took a step back as he approached. "I see I made a mistake by coming to you in the first place."

My mind raced. I was in over my head, and with what I'd shared with Ty, I risked my mom's and dad's lives too. I blinked the world back into focus, pulled from my tumultuous thoughts as the space between us shrank. He'd gotten a lot closer to me.

"Stop running from me." He swept me up in his arms and cradled me to him as he sat on the love seat. "What you told me about the explosion could help us. It sounds similar to the attacks against former SEALs on US soil. The same people who murdered your parents could also be the militia group that's sabotaging our missions. You won't be outed. I'm talking with my brothers about your *family*, not your parents. As far as everyone is concerned, you were born here, and your parents are alive. What I've said doesn't put you at the scene. And remember, my brothers are now your family too."

It took a while for my heart to calm and the anger to ebb. Minutes or maybe seconds ticked by while he waited for me to gain control of my emotions. When I could see without a red haze, I relaxed against him, most of the fight leaving my body. He was right. We'd lost men and civilians due to the leak on our team. Any details I had could help to save lives, including Ty's. "There's no way around this, is there? Whether I want to be or not, I'm the sacrificial lamb."

"You're my wife. I already told you that your battles are mine. We'll handle talking to my brothers about this carefully, but it's something we can't ignore."

I rested my head against his chest, breathing in his intoxicating scent. "My mom and dad—er, aunt and uncle—risked a lot to keep me hidden. I can't betray them."

"I understand who you're talking about. You don't need to call them 'aunt and uncle.' And you won't betray them. It'll work out. Trust me."

"I'm trying. Trust doesn't come easy to me." I'd bared my soul to him, so I figured a few more truths wouldn't hurt. "Beth was the first person I let get close and then Anna. It's not something I'm comfortable doing."

"We'll figure this out together, Lina." He smoothed the hair away from my cheek, sifting the strands through his fingers. "Or should I call you Gabriela?"

A sharp pain stabbed through my chest at hearing my former name on his lips. "No. I haven't answered to that name for a long time." I choked back emotion as the concerned expression Samuel had worn before mis padres had ushered him out of our house that evening flashed in my mind. In the space of seventy-two hours, I'd gone from Gabriela Malina Perez to Malina Gabriela Johansson, and almost two months ago, I'd become Malina Hale. It was a lot to digest, but taking Ty's last name would also muddy the waters of where I'd come from.

But he was right. If I could help save lives by telling his brothers about the explosion that killed mis padres, I would. "I understand why you want to tell them. Just… don't betray me, Ty."

His lips brushed across my forehead, and I let some of the tension ease from my body. "Now why would I do that? I went so far as to marry you in secret to keep you all to myself. Do you really think I'd chance losing you?"

"You did, and no." With a small smile curving my lips, I met his gaze. "Maybe there's hope for us after all."

A flare of desire turned his brown eyes almost black. "Never doubt it."

18

TYLER

Sweat coated my body as I slowed from a jog to a brisk walk along the shoreline. It was early, and shadows were elongated as the sun crested the horizon. That time of day was peaceful and invigorating. But with Malina's tempting body curled against mine, I'd had to force myself to get up and move. An hour before, I'd woken her to tell her I was going for a run. I almost didn't go.

The exercise had done a lot of good. Of course, Malina had consumed my thoughts for a majority of the run. When I'd first met her in high school, there had been something unapproachable about her, a steely toughness masking fragility and haunted eyes that stole my breath. That was a big reason why I hadn't dated her back then. I didn't want to destroy her even more.

I'd never forgotten about her.

When I became a SEAL, it had been a surprise to find her working as support to my team. She'd grown, matured, and healed. For me, nothing had changed. She was permanently imbedded in my psyche. Every time I saw her when I went on base, I couldn't tear my eyes away from her. The only way she gave me the time of day was if we verbally sparred. I had always wanted Malina. She was my endgame.

I slowed my walk along the final stretch of the beach to cool down before going inside to shower as my mind continued down memory lane.

When she'd agreed to go on a date with me last year, all my pent-up desire for her had come out, and I'd brought her back to the island. It had been too soon. She wasn't that kind of woman, and I'd known it but hadn't been able to help myself. That very long night when she'd fallen apart in my arms had been more than she'd been willing to commit to or face, and she'd blocked me from seeing her again. I knew what she was doing. She'd attributed our passion to a one-night stand, which was what she expected from me. Demanding that I take her home in the morning and refusing to go out again was a way to safeguard her heart—a heart that had been devastated by the deaths of her boyfriend and parents.

I'd meant what I told her the other day. There was no going back from that night, not for me. I'd always known she would be the one. In Vegas, with her walls down, I'd seen the answers I'd hoped for all along reflected in her beautiful eyes. It was a bit extreme, but I'd gone with my gut and asked her to marry me. She'd glowed, agreed, and flung her arms around me. In that moment, I never wanted to let her go. But when we woke the next morning, the old wariness had returned to her sleepy expression, and I slipped the ring from her finger.

I'd planned to tell her, to wear her down to date me, and I was genuinely surprised to find her on the island. But since we were finally on the same page, there was no way I would let anyone take her from me.

I turned from the shore and made my way to the screen door as the distant sound of a motor purred. Good. My brothers had gotten word to me that they were arriving that day. We had a lot to talk about and prepare for.

When I walked inside, the smell of coffee saturated the house, and I was drawn to her like a magnet. Her long rose-gold hair fell down her back in beachy waves that stopped just above her small waist. Tiny sleep shorts hugged her curves. I closed the distance between us then placed both hands on the island, caging her in. The scent of hibiscus surrounded me, mingling with the rich aroma of coffee beans. When she turned her head, I lost myself in her sleepy green eyes and shifted so that one of my hands rested on her flat stomach. I couldn't wait for it to swell with our child.

"Want some?" The corners of her lips twitched. "I settled for decaf, which is just wrong, but thankfully, you had some creamer. It sort of helped. I can make you regular if you'd like?"

I shook my head. "Later." Unable to resist touching her, I tucked a lock of hair behind her ear, trailing my fingers along the curve of her cheek. "My brothers are on their way."

Her fingers leeched of color as she gripped the mug tight. "What should I do? Hide?"

"No." I grinned despite the seriousness of her question. "They'll head to their homes first and drop off their luggage or whatever. I told them to come here when they're ready but without Riley and Kayla."

"Okay, yeah. That's good. The fewer people involved, the better."

My fingers wrapped around hers, gently freeing the coffee mug from her grasp. "Why don't you get dressed"—my heated gaze swept over her revealing clothes—"so I don't have to kill my brothers?" That earned me a real smile, and I shifted so that she could head to the bedroom and get ready.

A glass of water in hand, I went to the table and checked my messages. Still nothing from the Gray Ghost team, though I knew I would hear from them that day. My phone clattered to the table, and I rubbed my hands over my face as the gravity of the situation washed over me. I couldn't lose her. We had to uncover who the real mole was, the one who'd put us all at risk and killed both former and active SEALs. My guess was the same as hers. Mark.

I could hear the water turn on in our master bathroom and wished I could join her. Locking down thoughts of what I wanted to do with her, I forced myself to focus. The mission I'd been on, the hostage, and the cache of weapons replayed in my mind again as I searched for any additional clues that would help us.

It wasn't long before Xander and Jaxon entered. Malina was out of the shower, and the hum of the hair dryer drifted from our room. I'd filled them in about who was inside and the accusations against her so that they could make their decision about getting involved. Xander, the more laid-back of the three of us, plopped down in a chair. His recent marriage and honeymoon had obviously agreed with him. Jaxon planned on moving him and Riley into his island house full-time, as her parents were living in his Honolulu condo.

"It's your call if you want to be here or not," I said. "You know the risks."

"You're our brother. There isn't anything we wouldn't do for you," Jaxon replied, and Xander echoed his agreement.

"Let's get started, then." Their easy acceptance removed some of the weight from my shoulders. "We know based on intel from the last explosions on US soil that the Mahrib Allah militia group is suspected to be intertwined with the Venezuelan and Iranian presidents and behind the recent attacks. There was further proof of that during hostage captivity and the location of the weapons. I've already identified two of the members in the debriefing."

Xander leaned back in his chair. "But we're still missing who the leader is and their contact inside our team."

"There are theories." I didn't want to say it. "Mark was the one at Malina's workstation, helping the agents to locate the leak from her computer."

"What do we know about him aside from the fact that he went to school with us and has a possible gambling problem?" Jaxon stood and helped himself to coffee.

I shrugged. "There's not much I can offer. He's always been a bit of a loner. We know little of his home life, only that he was in the foster system. Over this past year, he seemed to get his life together. His relationship with Anna is solid, and I haven't heard much about trips to Vegas, so maybe the gambling has calmed down too?" Even saying that felt suspect.

"What's wrong with this coffee?" Jaxon stared at his mug with disgust.

I couldn't help from laugh. "It's decaf."

"Since when do you drink decaf?"

I shook my head. "Malina made it."

"Let's assume he is in over his head with gambling dept." Jaxon rejoined us at the table. "If he owes a significant amount of money, there is a possibility they got to him that way."

It was something that had been in the back of my mind the entire time, but I hadn't wanted to voice it. Mark was a friend, but I couldn't deny that he looked like the mole we'd been searching for. Before I could respond, my phone rang. I hit the speaker button, and after greeting Jack from the Gray Ghost team, I let him know my brothers were there and listening.

"I heard back from my contact today." Jack's commanding voice boomed through my phone's speaker. "You were right to question Mark. There is some suspicious activity."

"Anything that proves he's committed treason?" I couldn't believe I was asking that, but Malina's future hung in the balance. "Or that he recently came into money?"

"Funny you should say that," Jack answered. "We're following a thread surrounding a large debt that was paid to a known loan shark without any bank transactions."

It was a start but not enough. We needed to push things along, get Mark to make a mistake. A plan formed as I sagged back against my chair. If he saw Malina, he would likely make a move. Somehow, we would catch him. I didn't like it at all, but it was probably the best shot we had at causing him to slip up, unless I could lure him with a trip to Vegas and enough alcohol or an injection of a truth serum.

We finished up the call with Jack, and I met my brothers' eyes. Their features were set in grim lines by my reaction. I needed their aid. My teeth clenched and I cast my narrowed gaze their way. Everything would hinge on my plan working, and I needed their help.

They didn't know it yet, but my future was directly tied to Malina's.

19

TYLER

I'd tried to leave Malina home with either Riley or Kayla, but she wasn't having it. Determination similar to my own shone from her bright-green eyes. She was tiny but fierce, and I could deny her very little. Under the cover of night, we'd climbed into a speedboat and returned to my place in Honolulu.

As the boat rocked from the ocean's swells, she'd succumbed to fatigue and had fallen asleep in my arms. The feel of her against me had been torture, since I couldn't act on it. She'd stirred awake when we went from the marina to the truck and again from the vehicle to my condo. Reluctantly, I'd tucked her into bed, all wild hair and pure temptation. That woman could bring me to my knees with one touch—she just didn't realize it yet.

"Are we sure this will work?" Xander rapped his knuckles against the coffee table, drawing my attention from Malina and back to the reason we were there.

"It's Saturday, so he won't be at the office, and Mark never could resist going out." I'd called him the night before, asking him to meet us for a drink tomorrow, and baited the hook about another trip to Vegas. I could almost feel him salivating through the phone at the thought of it. Time seemed to move both quickly and slowly. We'd arrived in Honolulu in the darkness of early morning, but a glance at my phone told me it was afternoon. We had an hour before the meeting with Mark.

My brothers and I were going over the details of what we wanted to learn one more time as the door to my bedroom opened. Malina came out, wearing a loose deep-red spaghetti-strap shirt that both hugged and flowed around her body in such a mesmerizing manner that I stood and took a step toward her. Her gorgeous uniquely gold hair was down and in its usual messy waves. Sexy toned legs, visible from under her frayed denim miniskirt, had my mouth watering, and her strappy sandals revealed a pink pedicure. Her makeup was simple yet smoky. I lost my words for a moment. I wanted to lock her in the condo—she was too damn beautiful, and part of me worried she wouldn't stay with me even when the nightmare was finished.

"What're you doing?" I moved toward her. That invisible string drew me every time. Alarm had colored my words. *Why is she wearing sandals when she's supposed to remain here?* The woman would go barefoot everywhere if given the choice. She was an island girl at heart, the perfect one for me.

She lifted a slender shoulder then let it fall, the corner of her lips curving up in a mischievous grin. "I'm making an appearance at the bar too."

"The hell you are." Every muscle in my body went tight. The thought of Malina in danger terrified me.

"Wait." Jax stood and put a hand on my shoulder. "If she's visible then disappears, it could be enough to get Mark to make a move."

Malina winked then went into the kitchen for a glass of water. "I need this done, Ty. I can't deal with the stress."

Her plan wasn't good for her or the baby. It had actually been my first idea, but I'd dismissed it because I worried something would happen to her. I couldn't deny it was the best one, though. With a slight nod, I agreed to back off. But I had some hard and fast rules I was laying down first. "Xander and I will meet Mark. Jax, you'll be on hand to make sure Malina gets away without any problems."

"Wouldn't have it any other way," Jaxon said.

"She's—"

"A part of this," Malina cut me off.

I wanted to tell my brothers about the baby. She'd sensed it and stopped me, but they had to know everything that was at stake. They seemed to get that she was the one, probably because they had the women of their dreams, Riley and Kayla. But there was more to it. I would let them know without telling them directly. They needed to protect all of her.

I held Jaxon's gaze. "I want you waiting for her with a hat, sunglasses, and a change of clothes. She can't look the same when you leave the restaurant. And get her on the boat and back to the island." Xander and I would handle the recon from there.

Malina leaned on the kitchen peninsula. I stepped around Jaxon, and when I maneuvered behind her, she glanced over her shoulder. There was no fear, only determination. It was enough to ease some of the tension in my neck, and I pulled her to me and supported her back against my front.

I settled my hand over her stomach and shot my brothers a pointed stare, holding their gazes until their eyes went wide. Message received. Without saying it out loud, against her wishes, they understood that there was even more at stake.

20

TYLER

We stood on the edge of the bar and grill's patio, where Mark was to meet us. On a normal day, I loved it there. A pergola was strung with outdoor lights hanging on the wooden planks, along with several circling fans. The ambience encouraged people to stay. While it was a great place, every muscle in my body was tense, on alert.

Xander nudged my shoulder. "Relax. You look like you're ready to take down a target, not meet a friend."

I moved my head from side to side, cracking my neck. He was right. I was all kinds of wired, and Mark would pick up on it. "I don't like her being anywhere near here. She should be back on our island, safe."

"Jaxon will have eyes on her the entire time. She'll be on her way there before we even leave the bar."

She'd better be. There was too much at stake. "Let's grab a table."

The outdoor area was partially filled with only a handful of open tables to choose from. I gripped the back of a chair and pulled, but the sound of the legs scraping against the stone floor was lost amidst the chatter of the other patrons. Xander did the same, and we settled in to wait, our backs to where Lina would make a very brief appearance.

Xander smacked my shoulder, and I curled my hand into a fist, wanting to punch him. I moved my hands beneath the table to hide how they were still formed into fists. It wasn't normal for me, but I was off my game because of the risk to Malina.

We didn't have long to wait until Mark approached with his hand entwined with Anna's. He bent to her ear and whispered something that caused her to laugh. They embraced, and after a brief kiss, Anna went on her way. He remained there for a minute, watching her with longing before he turned toward us. Then recognition lit his face, and he lifted a hand in a wave before making his way to the table.

I stood and went to clap him on the back, my fingers deftly slipping a bug under his collar before I went back to my seat.

I tipped my head in the direction Anna had gone. "Things are looking serious." I forced an easygoing smile, or as much of one as I could.

"Yeah." Mark grinned. "She's incredible, and I have no idea what she's doing with me, but I'm going with it."

"Isn't that always the case? Hurry up and marry her before she wises up." Xander winked. "That's what I did."

"Jaxon plans to also, if I heard correctly." Mark half turned as the waitress approached. We all gave our orders.

"He does." I leaned back, my body deceptively relaxed. If he made one move to go to Lina when she made her appearance, I would intercept him. No way would he get within a foot of her. "Are you thinking about getting a place with Anna?"

The waitress appeared with our drinks, and Mark took a pull of his beer before answering. "Yes. We're moving in together at the start of the new year."

"That's not that far away." They must have been waiting for a lease to be up. "Anna didn't want to join us?"

"She had some shopping to do. I'm meeting up with her

after." His smile fell away. "I'm sorry about Malina, Ty. Anna told me you two are close. I mean"—he faltered, clearly uncomfortable—"I thought you didn't care for her, with all the bickering the two of you did, but Anna said otherwise. I'm sure it's been hard on you to know what she's done."

"Allegedly," Xander broke in. "Has she been brought in for questioning yet?"

I couldn't unlock my jaw, and every fiber of my being wanted to jump across the table and slam my fist into his face. With the small breather Xander had given me, I regained enough control to stay in the game.

"She ran." Mark took another drink before setting his beer down, his gaze doing a lazy sweep of the other tables. "If she didn't have anything to hide, why would she do that?"

"Has Anna talked to her?" I asked. "I know they're friends."

Mark stiffened, his sight locking on something, or someone, behind us. "No. She hasn't spoken to her since before the morning when the security leak was found."

Interesting. Malina must have made her appearance, but he hadn't said anything to us. He was definitely involved. *I wonder what Anna knows.* We would have to explore whether or not she suspected Mark as well, because according to Malina, Anna was the one who'd told her to run.

"Excuse me for a minute." Mark got up and maneuvered around us.

Xander and I turned when he was past us, and after a panicked check, I was able to breathe. Malina was nowhere to be seen. But Mark was headed toward where she would have gone, pulling his phone from his pocket. Jaxon was listening in via the Bluetooth connection to the bug I'd planted.

Malina had been correct. Her brief appearance was what we needed to force a move from Mark, hopefully taking us to his source. He had to have had help. The guy I knew from high school had always wanted to be accepted, and my fear was that he'd found it with the wrong people.

When Mark came back, I expected him to make an excuse to leave. We would be ready, though, because nothing would stop me from securing Malina's future.

21

MALINA

My appearance at the edge of the outdoor bar lasted only a few seconds, but it was enough. I felt Mark's gaze on me, and the fine hairs on my neck and arms stood at attention. As soon as I moved out of sight, Jaxon's hand clamped around my bicep, and he wrapped me in a long tan cardigan then yanked the hood up. A pair of sunglasses went on next. He rushed around the block at as brisk a pace as he could muster on the busy Honolulu sidewalks. We weren't far from the marina, which was why the guys had chosen that particular restaurant in the first place.

With each step, some of my anxiety over being out in the open faded. My little cameo was done, at least for the time being. I would do whatever it took if there were other opportunities.

We'd put some distance between us, but Jaxon urged me to go faster. I shouldn't have had that large glass of water before we'd left. Each step we took was like a hammer to my bladder. I had to stop and find a bathroom. The boat ride wouldn't be long, but there was no way I could last fifteen to twenty minutes.

The marina was ahead, and as soon as I saw the public restrooms, I tugged against Jaxon's hold. When he turned, I pointed at the building. "I need to use the restroom."

There was no one around the small structure, and the boat was only a few slips away. He set his mouth in a grim line but released me. "Come straight to the boat when you're done. I'll get it untied and the engine started."

"Okay." I pivoted and made a beeline for the women's bathrooms. I shoved my dark, tinted glasses on top of my head as soon as I entered the dim restroom. Inside the stall, the long cardigan went on the hook. After emptying my bladder, I washed my hands and splashed some water on my face, trying to chase away a sudden bout of exhaustion. The sunglasses slipped, and I set them on the edge of the sink. I took a moment to settle my nerves. Tyler and his brother's overprotectiveness was causing me to reach a whole new level of frazzled. Patting my face dry with a paper towel, I glanced in the mirror to assess the damage to my eye makeup when another woman walked in.

Oh, how weird. It was Anna, and my tension eased when I realized it was her and not someone else from work who might have turned me in. I had to get out of there and meet Jaxon.

With a grin, I turned to face her. "Hey. So strange. What are you doing at the marina?"

There was a hard glint in her dark eyes that I'd never seen before, and her lips pressed into a tight line. Then I saw a gun pointed at me, and things clicked into place. She'd told me to run while Mark led agents to my computer. They'd set the trap together.

"You and Mark set me up."

She shrugged. "Actually, Mark did when he discovered what I'd used his access code and computer for. It was either take the blame, plant the leak elsewhere, or watch as the woman he loved went to jail."

"Then you're taking both of us down." I gripped the edge of

the sink. "The investigation won't stop at me. They'll comb through every electronic impression you made."

She didn't seem phased.

"Oh God, you knew that. He was the one you meant to set up to take the fall. But he loves you. Why would you do that? I've seen you with him. You love him too. I know it. Please, Anna, think about what you're doing."

Her grip tightened on the gun, but I caught a tremor running through her arm. "I have thought about it. It's the right thing to do." She steadied the weapon. "I'm a soldier of Allah, and no sacrifice is too great."

22

TYLER

Mark was alone and on the move. The only way I could block everything out and focus on the mission was remembering that Jaxon would soon be on our island with Malina. She was safe.

There'd been a text from Jax that Mark had called someone named Nasir, and they were going to meet. That's all he'd gotten from the bug I'd placed.

Xander and I followed in his black F150 at a distance, keeping several cars between us. We were headed out of downtown Honolulu and to the outskirts of the city. "I know where he's going. You can ease up even more so he doesn't suspect us," I said.

The truck was a beast and would have been easy to spot for anyone looking. If Kayla's car hadn't been in the shop, we would have taken it, as it would have been more inconspicuous, but I didn't think Mark was paying all that much attention. He seemed focused, his head never shifting right or left unless he was crossing an intersection after a stop sign. Nor did I see him look in his mirrors except for obvious reasons.

I couldn't stop thinking about all the clues that I should have put together sooner. Maybe then he wouldn't have used Malina to take the fall for him.

For instance, there had been a time when Xander was dating Riley and we'd stopped to eat at a burger joint we frequented now and again. As we were leaving, we spotted Mark across the street at a mosque, talking to someone he later told us was a long-lost relative. I'd filed away the information because something hadn't added up with how the guy had looked at us. There'd been a narrowing of calculating eyes and something in his posture that had my instincts on high.

I hadn't pushed for details, as Mark had seemed genuine. But the man whom he'd claimed as family stuck with me, and I would have bet that was where he was headed.

That wasn't all that flashed through my mind as the clues clicked into place. Jaxon and I had once run into Mark at Pearl Harbor while we were on our way to visit Xander, who was being released from observation after a mission-related injury. Mark had bruising on his face and waved it off as a bar fight, but that could have been the loan shark's doing.

Xander dropped back another car length. It didn't take long until we were pulling into the parking lot across from the burger joint, which was for the modern mosque with its large domed peak. Mark claimed to have frequented it as a compromise to Anna. Once he was out of the car and heading in, Xander parked. We settled in to wait, two rows back with a good view of the front entrance where he had disappeared. His supposed relative could have been the connection we were looking for.

Xander broke the silence. "Any word from Jaxon?"

"No." I tried not to let it get to me. I was worried about Malina. When my phone rang, I pushed out a relieved breath but then saw that it wasn't Jaxon but Jack from the Gray Ghost team. I put him on speaker so Xander could listen. Jack got right down to why he called, which was something I'd always liked about him.

"We found something in Mark's background check. He was born in Iran, and his parents were killed in a bombing. Not long after, a relative moved him to Honolulu. When a robbery ended his guardian's life, Mark was put into foster care at the age of four after his uncle declined taking him in."

"We're looking at abandonment issues at the very least." Not surprising, but I'd hoped for more information. "Anything about other relatives?"

"This is where it gets interesting. He has a couple of cousins in Iran, including one who popped up on the government's radar, Nasir Jafari. We think he might be involved with the Mahrib Allah militia."

I wrapped up the call then placed one to the Navy's master-at-arms. We needed security and a way to apprehend him without frightening anyone inside other than our determined targets.

Five minutes later, Mark exited the building. His head was down, and he was texting as he walked. When he neared the first row of parked cars, we stepped out of the truck. He wasn't going anywhere.

2 3

TYLER

"What the hell, Tyler? I thought we were friends," Mark growled, his hands zip-tied behind his back and his gaze darting between Xander and me.

We'd converged on him after he'd left the mosque and strategically led him to an outside corner of the building just as a team arrived to take over for us, temporarily detaining all who were inside until we apprehended Nasir and figured out who else Mark worked with in there. He was obscured from sight in a secluded back corner against the outside of the structure.

He was a friend—or had been. All I could focus on was the mission and keeping Malina safe. "I'm asking the same thing. Why did you set up Malina, and who are your contacts?" I blocked out everything but the mission, which was to take down the terrorist cell that had infiltrated our ranks.

With a puff of air, he deflated against the brick, defeated. "You don't know what it's like."

"Explain it to us." I wanted fast answers, but so long as she was safe, I would take them any way I could.

"This isn't what I wanted, but to have someone who loves

me... it's everything. My life was different from yours." Resentment burned in his dark gaze. "Not everyone had parents like yours, a place to sleep that was safe."

"We know you were born in Iran, that you came over here when you were young, and that you lost your guardian in a robbery, leaving you orphaned."

"Yeah, that's the abridged version. One of my uncles brought me over, posing as my parent, something I recently found out. He wasn't my father but my mom's brother."

"How did you find this out? Who told you?" Xander asked.

"You're not focusing on what I went through after moving." Mark sneered at my brother. "I suffered. I had another uncle who lived here. I could have gone to him, but he disagreed with how my parents thought and looked at me as an extension of their ideals. He denied me a home, a safe place to rest my head at night. Do you know what it was like in the foster system?" His voice vibrated with emotion. "It wasn't always the foster parents. I slept with a rock under my pillow to defend myself from the other kids and sometimes the adults themselves, depending on which home I was in. No one looked too closely at what unwanted kids dealt with."

"That wasn't the question." Xander took a step closer, crowding him.

"Well, you're going to listen. Maybe then you'll understand." He paused, and we let him think he was in control. "Fast forward to my job supporting the SEALs, where I met Anna. But she was dating Kyle."

"So you had him killed?" Xander asked.

"No," Mark spat. "I waited, and when they broke up, I pursued her. And she was everything I'd ever hoped for."

"What does this have to do with betraying your country?"

"I didn't..." Frustration pulled Mark's features tight.

I eased back as Xander pushed Mark and observed. The

same zealous, obsessive look he got when gambling flashed in his eyes when he mentioned his girlfriend. It was enough for me to know exactly where the situation was headed. What we needed were names. His motivation was clear, and I was fine learning the how of it later. But if Mark was pushed to that point where he had nothing to lose, we might be able to get both.

My phone vibrated in my pocket. I ignored it, as we were close to getting the answers we needed. The team was in place; I caught a visual of Joe and a few others not far away.

Mark had yet to spot them. "Anna is everything to me. And she loves me as much as I do her."

"Did you have anything to do with Kyle's death?" I asked. We had to move it along.

Mark swung his gaze from Xander to me, horror clear in his stormy expression. "No. Why would I have done that. And how?"

I shrugged. "Anna had a soft spot for him, and it was well-known that the two of you didn't like each other, and that you both were after the same woman." I paused and stared at him. "You must have had something to do with the failed missions, the deaths of John and Kyle, because you led the investigation to Malina's computer. We both know it wasn't her that betrayed our country. We need names, Mark. Who are you working with? Is it the new family member you met when you started going here?" The image of Mark talking to that man flooded my mind. It had to have been Nasir.

Mark's shoulders slumped. "Nasir helped me to clear my gambling debt. He asked me to watch out for Anna, as if I wouldn't have protected her anyway. When I found out what she'd done, well, it was a small thing I did for them both in return." He lifted tortured eyes to meet mine. "I would do anything for the people I love."

THE VIBRATION from my phone was constant. Stepping away from Mark and Xander, I pulled it from my pocket, never taking my eyes from Mark. Jaxon's name lit up the screen. My heart skipped a beat when I answered.

"Malina is missing."

I tensed, gripping the phone tighter in my hand. "Explain how this happened." My worst fear, that she would be taken from me by the enemy or the government, had materialized. My muscles contracted into hardened determination. We had a weak link in Mark, and I planned to exploit it.

Jaxon's voice cut through the phone as he explained how Malina had gone to the restroom while he went to get the boat ready. Whoever had taken her did so through the back window. "I reviewed cameras pointed in the general direction of the bathroom. There was a crush of people heading to the marina after we split up for those few minutes, but no one stood out. I'm combing the area, but tell me that you've got something from Mark."

I wrapped up the call and stalked to where Xander leaned into Mark, interrogating him further. I bumped Xander over, curled my fists in Mark's shirt, and lifted him so that his feet dangled above the ground before slamming his back against the brick. Fear made his eyes wide, his pupils contracting to mere pinpricks.

"Where is she?" I growled.

"Who?" Mark's hands shot up, his palms defensively facing me.

"Malina. Who took her, and where is she?"

"I don't know." His voice quivered. "Nasir is the only person who might know something. I'm not in the loop. You have to believe me."

The problem was that I did. I dropped Mark so that he

regained his feet, swung him so that he was by my side, and fisted the back of his neck. By then, backup should have extracted Nasir and determined whether there was anyone else we needed to detain inside. I handed Mark over to the team. Before they took the prisoners away, I would have a heart-to-heart with Nasir.

2 4

MALINA

My heart slammed against my ribs in what felt like a desperate attempt to break free. I peered around Anna, but she'd locked the door to the restroom.

She waved her gun toward the frosted glass window set high in the wall. "We're going out the window. At the same time."

"Why?" *What am I doing? If I get to the ground before her, maybe I can escape.*

Her hand curled around my arm, and she backed me toward the wall. "Because if we go out the front door, Jaxon will see us." She pulled a roll of duct tape from her purse, tore off a piece, then slapped it over my mouth. I guessed there would be no screaming for help.

Sweat slicked my palms as we climbed up on the sink. Holding the gun steadily on me, she made me open the window and pop out the screen.

"At the same time." Her usual warm brown eyes were cold when she delivered her next statement. "Don't try to run. I will shoot you."

We each flung a leg over the metal frame. It bit into me as I positioned to turn so I could lower myself down the outside wall. We both dropped at the same time, and she shoved the gun into the small of my back.

"The car's over there."

I knew what car she drove. From where she'd parked, there wasn't a clear view from the boat Jaxon was getting ready for our getaway. I only hoped he was on his way to find me sooner rather than later and would spot us before she had a chance to take me away.

We arrived at her car, an early 2000 Lexus with rusted white paint, a model that was known to have defective emergency trunk releases. She popped the trunk and shoved me. I whirled around and gave her my best are-you-freaking-kidding-me expression.

"Get in."

The gun was pressed to my stomach, reminding me of all I had to lose. I did as she asked. The trunk was empty, with a clearly broken emergency pull handle and no handy crowbar or anything I could use as a weapon. When she shut me inside, I tore off the duct tape, ignoring the massive sting and my watering eyes. I opened my mouth to scream for help as she started the car and cranked up some bass-thumping rap music. Dammit! No one would hear me scream or kick the trunk with that noise.

While she drove, I kicked at the spot where one of the taillights should have been. If I could break through, someone would be sure to notice a random leg hanging out the back. We hadn't gone far when she stopped, and the only progress I'd made was making my foot sore.

The trunk popped open, and she hauled me out. We were inside a garage. Anna pressed the barrel of a gun to my back and forced me into the house through a connecting door. Scrapes covered my arms from our climb through the women's bathroom window, but that was the least of my worries. Betrayal sat heavily in my gut over someone whom

I'd thought was a good friend but instead was threatening my life.

My gaze darted around the sparsely furnished room. Wicker furniture decorated the space, with a small table off the kitchen and metal folding chairs around it. There weren't any other people that I could see, which gave me hope. I needed to keep her talking, to stall. If there was any chance to escape, I would take it. Distracting her was the best way, and I had a hunch I wanted to test.

"I get now that when you told me to run, you were solidifying my guilt. Does Mark know that you're the mole?"

Anna shoved me, waving the gun toward the table. "Sit there. Hands where I can see them."

After one glance at the linoleum table's questionable surface, I inched as far from it as possible. I shifted so that my body was turned to the side of the round table, enabling me to keep an eye on her as well. I did as she said, placing my hands on my thighs. "So that's a yes? Mark knows that you're the mole?" I needed the information because one way or another, I would escape.

She leaned against an ancient kitchen wall with wallpaper done in yellows and pale greens, a pensive expression crossing her features. I didn't recognize the woman before me. Gone was her sometimes joking and flirtatious nature, and in its place was a brainwashed soldier. I needed to talk to the woman I was friends with, not the chilling persona she presented.

She pursed her lips, and a flash of the old Anna shone through, however briefly. "He does. Why do you think he planted the email thread on your computer?"

I wasn't surprised. Mark was stupid in love with her to the point of blind devotion. At least, that was how it appeared when I caught him looking at her with puppy dog eyes when she was unaware. He managed to mask some of the obsession when she would catch his gaze in return. I'd always thought it was a bit creepy, but he wasn't really my friend but my superior, as I reported to him. Not anymore. I needed more truths from her. "Then he's a part of what you're involved in."

She gifted me a humorous smile. "Not fully, but he will be. What we're doing is important. And after Kyle died, Mark was grateful, in a way."

"What?" She'd stumbled over Kyle's name. That was a sore point, and maybe I could use that against her. "Look, I get that Mark and Kyle didn't get along, but to have him killed… that's going too far." I couldn't help the horror I felt. She was glossing over something appalling. "And how could you be okay with that? I know you still had feelings for Kyle."

"It was never meant to be. I shouldn't have let myself fall for Kyle. But I made amends. Mark is related to one of the leaders, so bringing him into the fold was necessary. The information leaked was important to the people I work with."

"Mahrib Allah? Is that who you're talking about?"

"You're asking too many questions. Be quiet, and I'll share with you what I can."

I nodded. There was nothing else I could do. She had a gun aimed at me, and I needed answers to give to Ty so he could stop the terrorist group she was a part of. It had to have been the militia he'd talked about to his brothers and the Gray Ghost guy.

"As a soldier of Allah, there's a bigger picture, Malina."

Whatever she was going to confess to me didn't happen when we heard the sound of a car pulling into the driveway. With her fellow soldiers' imminent arrival, I felt the jaws of death snapping at my heels.

Spots decorated the edge of my vision, and I swore the dingy walls of the cramped kitchen closed in. The image of the last day I saw my parents superimposed itself on the present, along with the same sense of urgency and the realization that things would never be the same. It was difficult to draw a full breath. That was where my fear of confinement had originated, with the awareness of freedom being stripped away and never seeing loved ones again. I was bound to come face-to-face with the people who held my fate in their hands.

It came sooner than I thought. Four men filed through the door, and my heart skyrocketed, slamming against my rib cage. Fear licked along my spine. I knew them. I saw them often in my nightmares. My gaze was riveted on one in particular, the same man who had been at the harbor when I fled to Ty's private island, the same man who had been sent to handle my parents. Dark eyes set in a hawklike face regarded me, and I fought from visibly trembling.

I tore my horrified gaze from his to Anna's, desperate for some sign of the woman whom I'd considered a friend. *Do they know who I am, or is this a horrible coincidence?* "Why are they here? Where's Mark?"

I knew the answer to one of those questions, but I wanted to hear it from Anna because I couldn't wrap my head around those militia men being in the same room with me.

The leader jerked his head to the right, communicating without words. She snapped to attention, and any warmth she had left her expression. Instead of responding, she yanked me from my seat and shoved my arms through a vest that was rigged with explosives.

Saliva pooled in my mouth, and I swallowed rapidly. It was that or throw up.

"Mark served his purpose." She kept her eyes averted while she nimbly fastened the death trap that hugged my body.

I caught a tremble in her fingers as she answered me. It was enough. She cared. *But can she be turned if we get away from the others?* I doubted it, but it was an angle I had to try to exploit.

The man from my nightmares snapped something in Arabic to Anna. She nodded then stepped back. He moved forward, and like the prey I was, I wanted to retreat, but there was nowhere to go. All the fine hairs on my body stood on end as he stopped in front of me, leaving mere inches of space. Even though it was just an intimidation tactic, I couldn't process it, couldn't overcome the irrational fear of what was happening. He had been the boogeyman in my dreams ever since I'd left Venezuela. I prayed Mom and Dad were far away. We'd thought I was safe. How wrong we had been.

He reached out and fingered a long strand of my hair. I jerked at the touch, the queasiness ratcheting up another notch. A close-lipped smile curved his thin mouth. "The one that got away."

Oh crap! They'd found me. There would be no running this time.

His voice was soft and oddly feminine. It sent chills skating along my bare arms.

"I don't know what you're talking about." It was a lie. We both knew it, but I'd be damned if I admitted anything to him. I was screwed no matter how I looked at it, but he still didn't deserve answers.

"You do." He barked orders in his language, and Anna and the men responded immediately. I was hustled to the door, where I caught a glimpse of a black minivan in the driveway. With deceptive gentleness, he lifted my hand and pressed the detonator switch into it. I jerked it back. Tears filled my eyes. His hand locked around my wrist in an iron grip. He placed the device against my palm, curled my fingers around it, and lined my thumb up over the top. A dark gleam entered his dead eyes as he applied pressure to my thumb over the switch.

There was an audible beep, and red numbers on a panel on the front of the vest began the count down. A whimper escaped my trembling lips, but I refused to fully break down. I had to stay sharp and look for a way out, even though it appeared there would not be one.

Wrapped in C4 explosives, my time was limited. Unless by some miracle Ty was able to save me, I would never see him again. The life we'd hoped we would have wouldn't exist. My heart wept, even though I refused to let a single tear fall in the presence of the man who'd murdered my parents and Samuel and had run me from my home in Venezuela.

Someone waved a cell phone in front of my face, and the man gave instructions to both me and his followers. Terror took hold of my mind as his words registered in its darkest recesses. There was no way out.

"We are, as Americans say, killing two birds with one stone. Goodbye, Senorita Perez."

Then we were outside, and someone hurried me to the van. The door slid open, and Anna shoved me inside then followed close behind. The door shut, and the other two got in the front.

Anna settled in one of the bucket seats beside me. "Anna," I whisper-yelled, "help me."

Her head dropped so that her chin rested on her chest, and she turned to me with unshed tears in her eyes. "I can't do that. I'm serving a higher purpose, and my orders are clear. We all make sacrifices, Lina. This is yours."

A spark of anger shot through me. "Was giving up Kyle then having him killed part of yours? Was converting Mark? What'll happen to him? To you?"

"It doesn't matter. Our fate is in Allah's hands."

The van lurched to a stop, and I realized we were inside the naval base at Pearl Harbor. The door opened, and Anna and one of the men from the front hauled me out. She issued parting words: "You have your instructions."

I stood there, shaking like a leaf and knowing it wouldn't be long before someone noticed me.

———

Tyler

WE WERE STILL in the parking lot of the mosque. Frustration at not knowing where Malina was, at being stuck there, answering questions, was causing my temper to snap.

"We'll find her." Xander clamped his hand on my shoulder and steered me away from the rest of the guys helping to secure Mark and clear the area.

Xander better be right. Fear for Malina ate at me, and I wanted to do serious damage to find out where she'd been taken.

Mark was hauled away before I permanently maimed him. An interrogation was in progress, but due to my personal involvement and willingness to do physical damage in public, I was not included in the process. He'd claimed not to know the rest of the plan. All he was to do was shield Anna's activities when he learned of them. Nasir had slipped out of the mosque before we surrounded it. There were only civilians inside, who were cleared to go.

It seemed fair to guess that Nasir had her. We had the full name confirmed by Mark, and a search was in progress for him, but that didn't diminish the hollow pit in my stomach. Nothing would until she was safe and in my arms.

The shrill sound of my phone ringing snapped me out of my dark thoughts. I answered while opening the driver's-side door to Xander's truck. I couldn't be a passenger just then.

"Where are you?" Daryl, my team leader, didn't bother with a greeting.

I rattled off our location, hoping he had good news for me.

"Get to the office. Malina is here."

"Is she okay?" There was no answer. Daryl had hung up after delivering the order. The truck roared to life, and I peeled out of the parking space.

"What did he say?" Xander shouted over the roar of the engine as we squealed around a tight corner.

"That Lina is on base. He didn't say anything else." I couldn't look at my brother. There was a very real possibility that he'd hung up because she didn't have long to live. I couldn't go there. I held fast to the goal of getting to her, staying laser focused on the fastest route.

We arrived at the base in half the time it should have taken. By some miracle, we managed to elude the police en route, and the guard waved us through, probably on an order from Daryl. It didn't look good. My heart was in my throat as I leapt out of the truck and sprinted to the building where the SEALs had meetings and our team's support staff worked.

The area was clear except for several men decked out in full protective gear and wielding handheld shields. Then I saw her a few feet from the entrance to the building, in the middle of a semicircle of men bracketing her from a good fifteen feet or so back. Tears streamed down her cheeks. All the air whooshed out of me at the sight of the vest strapped to her and her shaking hand with her thumb holding down the detonator switch.

Her voice carried to me on a slight breeze. "I didn't suspect her. I'm sorry, Ty. Sh-She reports to others."

"It's going to be okay." The acrid bitterness of bile filled my throat. It wasn't good. I let myself slip into mission mode, needing the focused calm to think. To save her. "Who is she?"

She took a stuttered breath, her eyes pleading with me and showing another unnamed emotion I didn't want to look too closely at because it looked like goodbye. "Anna."

Daryl's hand tightened on my bicep. I hadn't been aware he'd grabbed me. The sight of Lina shook me to my core.

"Malina was told to have you and your brothers come. We caught Anna as she was leaving the base." He spoke in low tones but paused at a commotion to our right. Several guards approached with caution. Two held on to Anna's upper arms, her hands cuffed in front of her. "Bring her here." Daryl motioned them forward.

"Why haven't they disarmed the bomb?" I matched his quiet voice, rushing the words before Anna was within hearing distance.

"David, our bomb expert, is ten minutes out. We're waiting for him. There's a secondary detonator, at the very least. We aren't sure if there are more. We think a phone is one of the activators. A signal kill switch is on the way, and then we'll approach and disarm."

Xander made his way over to me, but I addressed Daryl. "I'm going in."

"Ty!" Malina's panicked eyes met mine when she heard what I'd said to Daryl. "I forgot my umbrella."

Shit. Under my breath, I told Daryl to get my brothers away. She'd used the code words she'd told me about, which her parents had made her memorize when she was young. By saying that, she'd let me know that she was without protection and compromised, and that I wasn't safe. It was meant to get me to leave. I would send my brothers to safety, but there was no way I would go. We were in it together, no matter what.

TYLER

Thick, dark clouds flooded the sky and blocked the sun. An electrical charge piggybacked the trade winds, trailed by a bitter chill, as if the universe rallied against the injustice we faced. The need for action, to fight the invisible terrorists, roared deep inside my psyche, aligning all my actions and reactions in offensive readiness.

No matter what, I would save my wife and unborn child.

The guards released Anna into Daryl's custody on the off chance that we could extract information from her. I needed a goddamn miracle. Malina was all alone and terrified. My hands clenched at my sides with the need for action. I wanted so badly to hold her in my arms and make it all go away. There had to be another way.

Tearing my gaze from my wife, I crowded Anna. Her long dark hair was pulled back in a low ponytail, and defiance flashed in her brown eyes. The fanatical gleam had never been apparent before that moment. I wanted to strangle her and snap her slender neck. But there was another approach.

"We have Mark. He's in an interrogation room. I don't have

to tell you what I'll do to him or what my brothers will on my behalf."

Her bottom lip trembled before she pressed her mouth into a tight line.

"He won't die today, but he'll wish he had. You could help him."

She shook her head in a hard left to right.

I curled my hand around her index finger, blocking what I was about to do with my body. I bent it back until it reached the sweet spot where I could easily break it. "Tell me about the second detonator. Who controls it? How can it be shut off?"

Tears misted her eyes, but she tilted her chin up in stubborn defiance. "You're too late. There is nothing you can do to save her."

I applied pressure, and the snap of bone was subtle. Anna gasped but didn't utter another sound.

"Wrong answer." I gripped the next finger, repeating the same process, stopping just before the bone broke.

There was a good chance she knew nothing more, but I had to try. There was a countdown, and I needed that too. "Tell me everything you know. This is only the start of what will happen to you and to Mark, and you know it."

Fury caused color to flood her cheeks. "I only know my part in the plan. You know enough to understand that. Wire her then deliver her here. I was to return to the house. Await orders."

"You put her vest on, didn't you? Tell me about it."

She licked her lips, her eyes darting to Malina.

"She's your friend. And then there's Mark. You will be the cause of their deaths. Help me save them." Mark was on his own and at the mercy of whoever had him, but she didn't have to know that.

"There are wires under the vest too. There is a countdown timer, the phone, and also the thumb-depression detonator. There are three."

"We need to wait for David," Daryl cautioned.

Damn it. We couldn't hold off for the bomb expert. There wasn't enough time to wait even minutes. I shifted my tortured gaze from Malina to him. "I can't. She's my wife."

Shock traveled over Daryl's expression in a ripple effect before he got himself under control. "Understood." He barked out commands for one of the men standing closest to get me gear.

"I need a camera. Connect me to David." I knew him. He was damn good. If I gave him video feed, he could help me disarm the devices. Someone dropped a helmet with a camera onto my head. I pushed Anna into my team leader's arms. She was his problem.

Daryl pressed a roll of duct tape into my hand then grasped my arm to stop me. He transferred a set of tools to me then let go. Malina's entire body visibly shook, and she mouthed the word "no" as I approached. The men behind me had reported there were no snipers on the rooftops. The area had been combed then evacuated to a safe point beyond where the blast would reach. Jaxon was past that invisible line as well. From the updates gained through Daryl, Xander had joined the chase for the person who held the cell phone linked to her vest. He couldn't have been far.

The bomb expert was still ten minutes out. I couldn't wait any longer.

26

TYLER

With one hand, I gripped Malina's shoulder, holding a tool to cut wires in the other. David, our bomb expert, was synced via the video feed on my helmet and the two-way radio connected to my belt. A device that interrupted the frequency of cell signals was in use, which would eliminate one of the triggers for the bomb strapped around her.

Daryl had taped her thumb to the handheld trigger so she didn't inadvertently release the button, but I had extra tape just in case.

"Why didn't you listen?" Malina's whispered question contained the weight of her anguish.

I rubbed my thumb back and forth against her arm, trying to offer a little comfort. "We're in this together. Hold still so Dave can get a look at the way this thing is wired." I executed a circle around her, lifting her long hair so he had the entire view of the device strapped to her.

"There's a small capsule-sized box by her upper back. See it?" Dave's voice squawked from the speaker.

I rounded to where he indicated then waited for instruction. "Got it."

"Carefully open it and remove the transmitter."

Malina took a deep breath, and her body stilled, giving me a greater advantage to open the small compartment. It took seconds, and when it was out, a collective sigh could be heard from everyone present, though we weren't done by a long shot. Dave talked me through cutting the correct wires. With each one, a little light reentered her eyes. I winked at her despite the gravity of the situation. The stress was high, and that couldn't have been good for the baby. I wanted to take as much off her shoulders as I could.

Once I'd cut the last wire, Daryl had the men move even farther back. It was time to remove the vest. Mike and John approached with a steel box then left as quickly as they'd come. I waited another second, making sure the men were back and it was just Lina and me. "It's going to be okay. Trust me."

Her long hair fell forward, curtaining her face. "If we get out of this alive, I'm going with you to track him."

I released the first clasp, and she flinched when it clicked. When nothing happened, she met my gaze with steely determination.

"The one who ordered the bomb to be put on you?" I didn't want her within sight of the guy. "I thought it was Anna who did that."

"It was." She narrowed her eyes on me. "But you know just as well as I do that she's not the leader of the organization. Merely a soldier."

I released the next clasp, and she swayed before snapping her spine straight. The bottom connector held the most danger. There were wires that fed through each side. Disrupting the connection would set off the explosives if I hadn't severed the correct wires. Sweat coated my forehead as I squeezed the clasp.

Her hand covered mine. "I trust you."

The click was deafening, and as the vest sagged open, we both bent toward the metal containment chest. Carefully, we got her out of the rigged explosives, and I lowered it into the reinforced unit. Last was the trigger. I withdrew the electrical tape and tore off a section.

"How's your hand?"

She nibbled on her lower lip. "It's cramped."

That was to be expected, but it would also make it more difficult to have her ease her thumb back so I could slip the tape over the trigger and keep it depressed without the weight of her hand.

Feet pounded against the pavement, and we both looked up. Daryl was by our side with a thin screwdriver in hand. "She won't be able to do it smoothly."

With the cramping, her hand's mobility was compromised. His help meant everything. I gave him a quick nod.

He grunted. "As if I would let you do this all on your own."

I didn't say it, but I was grateful. Daryl wrapped his hand around hers then slipped the flat edge of the screwdriver under the pad of her thumb. When it was halfway under, I helped her ease her finger back. The switch held. When she was clear, I secured half of the button with tape.

"Step back, Malina." I tore another strip off but waited for her to move back.

"No." She lifted her chin. "We're in this together."

Not when her and the baby's safety was at risk. "Mali—"

"That's an order," Daryl snapped.

Her eyes flashed fire, but she stepped back. I had never been so glad to have him on my side. When she was at a safe distance, he inched the screwdriver head back. When it was clear enough, I replaced it with tape and carefully put the switch inside the container. It would remain there until Dave arrived to ensure it was disarmed correctly and removed it from the property.

I'd never felt such a range of emotions on a mission. The thought of harm coming to her... Daryl and I hurried from the chest and over to where she and the others stood. "We'll go to the hospital, get you checked out."

She shook her head, the stubborn expression never leaving her face. "I told you before that I was going with you. I saw their faces. I can identify them."

Daryl's head snapped up, and he flashed me a grim frown before addressing Malina. "Get with a sketch artist. Once that's done, you can help Tyler comb through the train station video to see if you recognize them."

"I'll meet with the artist, but I want to go to the marina. I have a hunch."

MALINA

I rubbed a hand over my tired eyes, leaving the sketch artist in the conference room. They'd run a scan on the image against people close to the Venezuelan and Iranian president and found it was a near match for a man known as Hashem Jafari. He had the same last name as Nasir, Mark's newly discovered cousin. It wasn't an uncommon name but one to look into as to discover if there was any relation between Hashem and Mark. If so, we needed to know how Mark actually fit into the militia's plans.

The door shut behind me with a soft click, and I walked into Ty's waiting embrace. The manhunt wasn't over, but in light of recent events, I'd been cleared of suspicion.

I absorbed the heat coming off his body and relaxed as he wrapped an arm tightly around me. He slid a hand into my hair and massaged the back of my head. I could slip into sleep right there and then if not for the job we both needed to do, the one I was sure he'd try to shut me out of again.

"That was the single most terrifying thing I've ever gone through, Malina. If anything happened to you—"

"Don't." I pulled back, meeting his gaze. "Nothing did. You

disarmed the bomb, and aside from the fear and adrenaline, I'm okay."

Small lines formed around his mouth. I reached up and smoothed a hand over his forehead, down the side of his square jaw, over the five-o'clock shadow that dusted his face, and ended up cupping the back of his neck. "I'm safe because of you and the team, but I won't be for long if we don't catch this guy. I'm a loose end, one he won't let live."

He dropped his forehead to mine. "I know, but it's not safe for you to go with me. You should stay here with a contingent of men guarding you. Out there, I can't control every variable."

"No, but I'll be with you, and that's the best-case scenario for my safety. You won't let anything happen to me. I'll be careful." I squeezed the back of his neck. "Let's go before he slips away."

"Let's do this." As he drew back, he grabbed my hand. "We need to get suited up and grab my brothers. Then we'll comb the harbor for signs of Hashem."

———

Tyler

THE FAMILIAR SOUNDS of the marina provided a sonic backdrop for the four of us as we prowled along the boardwalk. Xander and Jaxon positioned themselves on either side of Malina while I took point. Nothing could happen to her. Having my brothers with me was the only way I was even a little okay with her coming. But she was right. If we didn't find Venezuela's militia leader, her life, not to mention countless civilians' lives, would always be in danger.

There were no shadows for us to blend in to. We were out in the open and would be easy to spot, sporting Kevlar vests and with guns at the ready. Fortunately, there weren't as many people as usual due to the rolling gray clouds and thunder rumbling in the distance. We were headed to the harbormaster, who would know of any recent boats docked.

Boats were coming in, but none were going out. The waves jostled those already secured. The weather would have bought us time. My gut said the guy was there. We just needed to ferret him out.

Malina's hand pressed against my back, and I slowed when she tapped her finger.

"Keep walking. I'm going to drop back and chat with Hank." Her voice was whisper soft as she withdrew her hand. I felt her slow her pace behind me, that invisible thread we seemed to have connecting us stretching and fraying my nerves with the distance.

There was no way we would leave her unprotected. I gave my brothers a look, and we fanned out in a semicircle with our backs to Lina, who crouched beside an old man leaning against a palm tree. I'd seen him countless times before. He ran a fishing boat rental. From the corner of my eye, I took in his weathered exterior. His white beard was scraggly, and he had pushed thick, gray hair, long enough to end at the top of his open-collared Hawaiian shirt, back from his face. The deep tan helped him blend in, but his eyes gave him away. Intelligence crackled in their dark depths. And while his posture seemed casual, I didn't doubt for one second that he would spring into action if he chose to.

The questions were how Malina knew him and who he really was. Jaxon caught my eye with a knowing glance. I wasn't alone in my assessment. As a unit, we took a collective step back, forming a tighter circle around them. I angled my head so I could hear what she was saying.

"The day I left, there were three men walking along the boardwalk. The one slightly in front was of Iranian descent with a sharp nose. Tall and thin with a dangerous presence. I think he had on a dark-gray button-down and black slacks."

"He and the others are on the *Raptor*." Hank leaned closer to Malina. "Stay here with me. Let them go after him."

"You trust him?" I addressed my question to Malina but glared at the older man with a promise of what I would do if harm befell her.

Hank smirked. "She's safer with me than with the lot of you."

"Stop." With a roll of her eyes, she reprimanded Hank. "I've known Hank for years. We'll keep watch from here."

Even with her confident words, the terror of earlier had taken a toll. Exhaustion bled from her in waves, and I was grateful that the older man was there to keep her company. But I didn't know him. With a jerk of my head, Xander shifted back and took position by leaning against the tree. Hank huffed his disapproval. It didn't matter—the only thing that did was Lina's safety.

Jax and I did a sweep of the area before making our way to the cruiser docked two ships over with the bold name of *Raptor* scrawled across its port side. No one was on deck, and it appeared deserted, but Hank confirmed it wasn't. We had to assume they would see us coming. With that in mind, we sprinted the rest of the way. At the front of the boat, we crouched to avoid a direct line of sight from the windows.

A plank wasn't out, so we would have to jump the short distance to the rail. There was no way to board without them knowing. Jax squeezed my shoulder, and then we leapt for the side, quickly scaling up. When our feet hit the deck, we drew our guns and led with them.

I wasn't waiting for them to come up from the lower deck and did a quick check to make sure the stairway was clear. Back on the side, I crept down the stairs, the gun an extension of my arm, my finger securely on the trigger.

Movement had me increasing my speed. Two steps to go. A

man rounded the side, entering the stairwell. Shots fired. I ducked. Jax jerked to the side. We returned fire. One round to the chest. One to the head. Bullets whirled past us, piercing the opposite wall. Jax fell below the line of fire. I dove onto the dead guy at the base of the stairwell. My shoulder slammed into the human cushion, gun extended to the side, returning fire.

I unloaded my clip into the second target. Jax thumped behind me, covering my back. There was one more down there.

"Drop the weapon!" Jax roared.

I gained my feet, swiveling to provide cover. Jax kept his gun on the target. I took in the man's features. It was the guy Malina said was the leader. "Drop the weapon."

He was going to shoot. I could see it in his eyes. With a squeeze of the trigger, I hit him in the thigh. Mouth pressed in a tight line, the target dropped his 9mm.

"Kick it over here," Jax ordered, holding position.

I stepped over Jax and approached. His jaw ticked. Then his hand went behind his back, and Jax fired. Shoulder hit. Not fatal.

Stowing my weapon behind my back, I slammed my fist into the side of his face. "That's for touching what's mine, asshole."

His head snapped back, and I fisted his shirt, whirling him around. I shoved him against the side of the boat. There was a gun tucked into the back of his jeans, which I removed, placed on the ground, then kicked away. Jax came over and zip-tied his hands behind him. We did a weapons check and found a knife and another gun strapped to his ankle.

Once he was secured, I tossed him against a bench, and his side hit the table in front of it. A cruel grin stretched his thin lips. "My son will finish what I could not."

Fury raced through me, and I could guess what was coming next. Before Jaxon could stop me, I slammed my fist into the side of his jaw. His eyes rolled back in his head, and he slumped against the cushions, out cold.

If he'd said anything more about Malina, I wasn't sure I could have stopped myself from killing him. Jax stayed by our prisoner, guarding him for when he woke. The sound of Velcro filled the quiet when I pulled my phone from the small pocket. Pressing the number for Daryl, I gave him the details then hung up. "They'll be here in fifteen minutes." We had just enough time to get a good look around. There was a definite lived-in feel to the lower deck. Half-eaten cartons of food littered the table. We must have interrupted dinner.

We would do a more thorough search when the team arrived, but I wanted to do a preliminary one first. I swept through the bedrooms and didn't find anything out of the ordinary until I opened a large compartment behind the stairs. Several drones were secured on open shelves. A black duffel held another. They were store-bought with modifications that fit explosive devices. It was the tie-in to the recent bombings of the former SEAL team members and immediate family we were hoping to find.

The pounding of footsteps came from overhead. I rounded the stairs with my gun raised. Daryl announced his presence before he cleared the opening, and I lowered my arm then holstered my weapon. He wore his usual no-nonsense expression as he jogged down. I stepped aside. When he entered the lower level, he took in the two dead bodies and the third slumped over on the bench seat in the kitchenette.

"All dead?" he asked.

I shook my head. "Did you pass Malina on the dock?"

"Yeah. She's fine. You're clear to go. We'll handle it from here."

I clapped him on the shoulder. "Thanks. I'll be in later for the debriefing. Check the area behind the stairs."

Daryl barked out orders as Jax and I got the hell out of there. If the guy had woken, I didn't know what I would've done. My team lead understood. Despite Daryl and Xander's rocky start, I had a good relationship with him. He and Xander had had an understandable beef before when Daryl had stolen his girlfriend, Carly, but they'd since come to terms with what had happened. There wasn't any bad blood between us, and I was glad to serve under Daryl. In the end, it'd all worked out. After all, Xander had Riley now.

The dark clouds had moved away, under the influence of the trade winds, which brought in lighter but still dense replacements. I blinked, adjusting to being above deck. In two strides, I was at the side of the boat. With a short leap, my feet hit the dock. Jaxon was right behind me. He gained my side, and we hurried to where Malina waited.

Jax slapped a hand on my back, and a grin stretched my mouth. Malina sat opposite Hank, a chessboard between the two.

"We got him," I said.

Her head jerked up, and a sunny smile turned her face from beautiful to stunning in two seconds flat. I had her in my arms before she could say a word. My heart couldn't take the stress of worrying about her safety. I was never letting her go.

TYLER

Malina and I sat on a love seat in the doctor's waiting room, my arm wrapped around her, pressing her firmly to my side. They'd squeezed her in. I wasn't sure I would be able to physically release her when it was her turn to see the doctor. The day had been horrifying, and I had to keep touching her to make sure she was alive and safe. I couldn't lose her. All the games we had played were done. We were finally where we were supposed to be in our relationship.

The room was decorated in nauseating shades of mauve and blue. Family magazines, with a scattering of *Highlights* and *People* for good measure, were stacked in rows in hanging racks. We were both too keyed up to read. It felt like we were waiting for a different bomb to go off. She'd assured me she was fine, but until I heard the words from the doc that she and the baby were indeed one hundred percent healthy, I couldn't let go of the raging worry that they weren't.

There were a handful of very pregnant women seated around the room. Some had their husbands with them, and a few did not. After they got over the initial, obvious shock of seeing us in tactical gear, they cast Lina knowing looks and glanced at how tightly she was bound to me. I got it. I was being overprotective. But I had a right to be, given how I'd almost lost her.

The door that separated the waiting room from the doctors' offices opened, and a nurse with a mass of long, thin braids came out, holding a chart. "Malina Hale?"

"Yes," Lina responded.

I stood but maintained the tight hold I had on her. She squeaked, and several of the women in the room giggled. The nurse wore a huge grin, her shoulders shaking in laughter.

"Ty!" Lina slapped a hand against me chest, her voice a growl. "Put me down."

I scowled back at her as I took inventory of what she was mad about. I'd stood with her against my side, and her feet dangled a foot from the ground. Green eyes flashed fire as she glared at me while her cheeks turned pink. I shifted and slipped my other arm beneath her legs to cradle her to me.

"Oh my God, Ty!" Lina flung her head back and went limp against me. She crossed her arms over her chest and huffed out a breath. "I'm fine. Promise."

I grunted, as her statement didn't need a response. I wanted to hear an all clear from the doc. The nurse got herself under control and ushered us beyond the door and into an exam room.

"My name is Shirley, and I'll be your nurse today. You can set your wife on the examining table. I'm going to take her vitals, and the doctor will be in shortly."

I helped Malina remove the Kevlar vest before the nurse took her vitals. There were two chairs in the exam room, but I stayed by her side instead. As soon as we got some answers, I was getting her out of there and taking her back to the island. I needed some serious decompressing time with her.

It didn't take long for the doctor to enter. She extended her hand first to Malina then to me. "I'm Doctor Santos. It's nice to meet you both." She took a moment to go over the notes. "Looks like you're about two months along. Still in the first trimester. How have you been feeling?"

Malina slipped her hand into mine, and some of the tension eased from between my shoulders.

"I've been fine except for some nausea in the morning." She glanced at me, her gaze questioning.

"She was under a tremendous amount of stress today."

The doc's gaze roamed over my vest and then to the much smaller one that Malina had worn, which I'd draped over one of the chairs. "Can you tell me what happened?"

I shook my head. As a military doctor, she understood when things were classified.

"Well, let's take a look and see how the baby is doing." She flashed us a smile meant to reassure. The nurse reentered the room with an ultrasound machine. The doc lifted Malina's shirt enough to reveal her still-flat stomach and helped her to shimmy her leggings down a little. Then she squirted some gelatinous stuff on Malina's stomach and put a wand attached to the machine just below her belly button.

The doc clicked a few things on the keyboard before she shifted the angle so we could see. Then she turned up the sound, and a fast thumping filled the room. Malina gasped, her hand tightening even more on mine. The monitor showed the baby, which was the size of a kidney bean. Holy hell. I couldn't believe it.

Malina peppered the doc with questions about the baby and the different stages of development. Once I heard that both she and the baby were healthy, I tuned most of it out and focused on wanting to get her back home, where she could rest. The nurse printed some pictures, and after the doc gave her a prescription for prenatal vitamins, we made the next appointment and were out the door.

I couldn't get her into the truck quickly enough. She stayed close, seemingly okay with my hovering tendencies. That morning had scared the hell out of both of us.

We picked up the prescription and some groceries then headed to my condo. "I have to go to the base for a meeting in an hour," I said. "Xander and Jaxon will be here until I get back."

"Okay, that sounds good." She flashed me a smile but was distracted by the ultrasound picture held with care between her fingers.

We pulled into the parking lot. I parked, killed the engine, then went around and opened her door for her. We walked hand in hand to the elevator and rode it in silence to our floor. When we entered the condo, my brothers were in the kitchen, making food. I waved to them before pulling Malina out onto the lanai. I sat on one of the chairs and drew her across my lap, burying my head into the crook of her neck.

She ran her hands through my hair, and if I'd had the time, I probably would have fallen asleep that way. But we couldn't stay wrapped in a peaceful bubble like I wanted. I lifted my head to gauge her expression. "I've got to go to that meeting. You'll be okay?"

"Of course." She rolled her eyes, and I couldn't help but grin back at her. "We got to see our baby," she said with wonder.

"Everything got real in that moment. It was before, but to see her or him…"

"It's a girl."

I grinned at her. Boy or girl, it didn't matter to me. I was beyond happy the baby was okay. And the doc didn't tell us what the sex was, but there was something in the way Malina looked at me that made me believe she had a way of knowing. I wasn't going to question her. I'd seen crazier things.

I took in her long hair and its mixture of rose gold and lighter hues then her stunning almond-shaped green eyes. She was gorgeous and unforgettable, and I hoped our daughter took after her mother in both looks and personality—she kept me in check and challenged me at every turn. I loved the woman like crazy and was so happy that our drunken night in Vegas had resulted in all it had.

"We need to talk about the next year. While I'm gone, think about where you want to live. We can stay here in the city or on our island."

She lay her hand against my chest. "I don't need to think about it. I want to go to the island. But you're keeping the condo, right?"

"Yeah, definitely."

"Good. Because I'll want to be here in the last month. It seems like it would be easier to get to the doctor. I'd rather not risk traveling by water when I'm in labor."

There were many changes coming, and I didn't want to be gone for long lengths of time. I understood why Xander had made the decision not to re-up. I was going to do the same. "I have a year left with the SEAL team. When it's over, I'm not re-upping. I'll do what my brothers do and work with the Gray Ghost team on an as-needed basis and build up the custom-surfboard business."

"That sounds fantastic, but, Ty, you don't have to give up being a SEAL for me. I support whatever makes you happy."

I brushed a kiss across her lips. It wasn't enough, but it had to be. I couldn't be late. "I'll be back as soon as I can. Xander and Jax will be here the entire time."

"I'm not worried." She stifled a yawn with her hand then pointed to another chair. "But I'm going to take a nap out here on that lounger."

I stood with her in my arms and carried her to the one she wanted to sleep on. The air was warm and salty. The waves were too far away to hear clearly, but we had a fantastic view of the ocean. I set her on the cushion and kissed her forehead. "I love you."

She tilted her head up and gifted me with a tired smile. "I love you too, Ty. Hurry back."

I always would.

———

THE MOOD WAS both grim and relieved at the conference-room table with my SEAL brothers. Daryl led the meeting, pulling up several photographs of what was found on the boat Jax had secured.

"Based on digital documentation, we unencrypted the drones loaded with explosives, we were able to tie the leader of the Mahrib Allah to the deaths of our SEALs and the three former SEALs and their wives. We've also identified several other members of the militia."

"When will we go after them?" I wanted them all eradicated. It was a threat we couldn't let go. Other SEALs had been targeted, including my dad.

"We'll get to that another day. For now, we're locating and monitoring the remaining members." Daryl rubbed his hand over his forehead, looking as exhausted as I felt. "The leader of the militia, known as Hashem Jafari, was the man captured on *The Raptor*. Because of the comment he made about his son finishing what he started, we had a DNA test run to see if a match popped up. One did."

"Was it the guy we caught with the cell phone meant to detonate the bomb strapped to Malina?" Joe asked.

He meant Nasir Jafari. I understood why Joe thought Hashem might have been his father because I had the same inkling.

"No. They're related, but he's not the son." Daryl frowned. "It was Mark."

"Where is he?" Ice infused my veins. Any loyalty that

remained for the guy I'd known since high school shattered. He was a threat to too many people I loved.

"He's undergoing interrogation. We don't have reason to believe he had any contact with his father, but we can't be sure. Nasir, Mark's cousin and the only connection to the militia besides Anna, is still under investigation. As soon as I know something, we all will."

It wouldn't be over until they were all six feet under.

MALINA

With the sun at my back and a virgin piña colada in hand, I stood waist-deep in the ocean with Riley and Kayla. My toes curled into the sandbar as lapping waves caused me to sway back and forth in our semicircle. We faced the island's beach, where Ty and his brothers tossed a Frisbee to each other with one hand, while they holding held a beer in the other.

It was a gorgeous day. There wasn't a cloud in the midday sky, and the always present wind took the edge off getting overheated by the sun's intense rays.

Nothing could make me feel bad, not even the news we'd gotten the other day about Hashem, the leader of the small militia group, being Mark's dad. Daryl had said that the news broke Mark. After an intense interrogation, it was clear that Mark had no knowledge of Hashem or the doings of Mahrib Allah, aside from the damning evidence he'd found from Anna using his computer, evidence he'd then transferred to mine.

He was to go through intense therapy, getting the help he needed while serving time. His sentence was lessened, as he willingly aided in the investigation. Anna, Nasir, and Hashem weren't so lucky.

Ty and I would talk about Mark more when there was some distance between what had happened, the betrayal, and Anna kidnapping me. But that was all for another day. In the meantime, I wanted to enjoy being with my new family. I took in the beach then let Riley and Kayla's voices penetrate my awareness while they chatted about the custom-surfboard business and our roles in it. My gaze bounced between the two. It was exciting that we were starting a company. Nothing was set in stone about who would do what, but it was obvious that Riley, a professional photographer, would handle all the photography. Kayla had competed professionally, even at Pike, and would be in many of the shots.

I remembered her from high school. We'd had a moment once when we bumped into one another in the hallway. It lasted only a second, but I had been instinctively drawn to her. We had a shared experience of grief, and in that brief moment of recognition, I hadn't felt so alone. But we were part of different crowds and had never sought each other out. It was one of those things. It was nice to recognize I wasn't alone in my pain, but I didn't know that I wanted to commiserate with anyone either.

She'd lost her brother, and I mis padres and Samuel. Neither of us wore pain as a shield any longer—we were on the path to healing. I could sense that she was farther along that road than I was.

Kayla laughed at something Riley said, her smile wide and her green eyes sparkling. The sound was so infectious that I couldn't help but grin along with her. Riley tucked a strand of dark hair behind her ear before shifting her focus from Kayla to me.

"How are you feeling?" Riley's cognac-colored gaze locked on me.

I shrugged. "Better, I guess. Everything is still a little surreal."

"I bet." Kayla snorted. "You've had a secret wedding that you didn't even know about and a surprise pregnancy. If that wasn't enough, your life got a total upheaval with the accusations and kidnapping. Which inevitably brought you here"—she winked—"with us."

"Well, living here with all of you isn't a hardship."

"It'll be nice to have a new baby." Riley's expression was wistful.

Kayla's eyebrows climbed her forehead. "Are you guys thinking about having a baby too?"

"Not yet." Riley swirled her fingers in a semicircle through the water. "But I wouldn't mind starting a family. Our kids will have a different childhood than what I had."

"And they'll have each other." The thought of my child growing up and playing with theirs was a happy one. I hoped they jumped on the bandwagon soon. "Don't wait too long to start. It would be nice to have them all close in age."

Kayla wrapped her fingers around my wrist and gave it a squeeze. "And all the trying won't be a hardship either. I'd better give Jaxon a heads-up. We have some practicing to do."

Riley shook her head, and I couldn't help but laugh. Kayla waded toward the shore, quoting Meg Ryan from *Top Gun* and yelling, "Hey, Jaxon, you big stud!"

He responded with Goose's line: "That's me, honey."

Kayla laughed, breaking into a jog to get to the shore and his open arms. "Take me to bed or lose me forever."

"Show me the way home." Jaxon caught her up in his arms and carried her down the beach to their home, the chorus of our hoots egging them on.

I'd always thought of Xander as the laid-back, playful one and Jaxon as authoritative and serious. But Kayla brought out another side to him, and it was fun to watch them interact.

Over the couple days I'd gotten to know Riley and Kayla, I'd found friends and family, and I hadn't known how badly I'd needed them. Mom and Dad were back and would arrive tomorrow, along with Kayla's and Ty's parents.

Ty and I had decided to renew our vows with family and without the influence of alcohol. Kayla and Jaxon were also getting married. Butterflies danced through my stomach, and I spread my hand over my abdomen. I wasn't showing yet, but I would soon.

From across the water, Ty caught my gaze with a smoldering intensity. Bubbles tickled in my stomach. "Oh!" I grabbed Riley's arm but maintained the connection with Ty. "I think I felt the baby."

"That's so exciting." Her arm came around for a side hug. "What did it feel like?"

I grinned. "Like bubbles."

Riley mirrored my grin. "Let's head in. The guys look like they're about to come get us."

"Yeah, good plan." We had a long day the next day, and I needed some time alone with Ty that night. It was close to dinner anyway.

Xander and Ty helped Riley and me pick up the beach towels and the rest of the stuff we'd brought to hang out together. We waved goodbye to them, and I turned to Ty with an ear-to-ear grin. I couldn't contain how happy I was. He caught me up in his arms, and I looped my hands behind his head.

"What's going on?" His voice was a deep purr, dancing along my skin.

"Nothing." I toyed with the edges of his hair. "Just that I love it here with you. I couldn't be happier."

He lifted me higher, and I wrapped my legs around his waist. "Are you ready for our parents to come here?"

"Yeah." I really was. "Are you sure Mom and Dad should stay at your parents' place with them and Kayla's parents? Maybe we should have mine here instead."

"It'll be fine. Besides, their place is bigger. But if you decide you want them closer, we can put them in the guest room."

"Thanks. I'll talk with them tonight to see what they want to do." I contentedly snuggled into his embrace. His fingers combed through my hair in a soothing motion that was going to have me nodding off. In all the time I'd known Tyler, I'd never thought my heart would be safe with him. I couldn't have been more wrong. I knew the man would do anything for me, and I for him.

He pressed a kiss to the top of my head then whispered into the salty strands, "I love you, Malina Hale."

I had enough energy to respond with a heartfelt "I love you too."

The waves rolled, breaking against the shore, and the sun sat low in the sky. We were on the lanai, enjoying the warm breeze and ambiance. I knew I was going to fall asleep but that he would wake me for dinner. Afterwards, I had plans to say a few movie lines of my own that were bound to lead to what I was too tired to do before a nap.

But there was time. "This is paradise," I managed to whisper.

"You're my paradise." His deep baritone sent a wave of desire through me. He'd misunderstood what I'd said. I would have to show him as soon as I was able to lift my head from where I nestled in the crook of his shoulder. *How did I ever get so lucky?*

I never thought I would have a love like the one he showered me with. The island was nice, but *Ty* was my paradise.

Keep reading with the next chapter for a sneak peak of Broken Circle, book one in the Gray Ghost romantic suspense thriller series.

The End

———

Keep reading with the next chapter for a sneak peak of Broken Circle, book one in the Gray Ghost romantic suspense thriller series.
https://amymckinleyauthor.com/gray-ghost-series/

———

Keep up with Amy's releases by joining her newsletter:
http://eepurl.com/dEBqJn

———

Liv

SECRETS HAD the power to destroy, and Liv's could very well detonate her marriage. Still, she had to tell someone. Keeping the news from Alex wasn't her goal, and she would share it with him, just not yet. The elevator dinged, and Liv stepped inside, on her way to meet her best friend, Rachel, for lunch.

Her spirits lifted as she threaded her way through the crowded Manhattan sidewalk and drew nearer to the café. Weaving in and out to avoid a group of people to her left, she picked up her pace, ignoring the light bumps and jostles from the too-close pedestrians. A hard clip to her shoulder half spun her, and she stumble-stepped back.

The same man who'd bumped her shot his arm out to steady her. She blinked rapidly and dropped her gaze from his cold, tan features to where his hand tightly held her arm. *A butterfly tattoo?* Before she could study the mark further, he released her and strode away, the crowd swallowing him from her view.

With a shrug, Liv let the random incident slide from her thoughts. The restaurant was only a few feet away. The click of her heels echoed along the pavement. She spotted Rachel and gave a breezy wave then flashed a smile at the host as she bypassed him.

Rachel leapt up and pulled Liv in for a hug before they took their seats. The pungent smell of Stargazer lilies, which sat on the center of their table, churned her temperamental stomach. Intermittent stirrings of nausea had plagued her the past week. She motioned to the waiter and had him take the flowers away before they placed their order for salads and drinks.

Across from her, Rachel grinned. "Did you survive 'the event of the season'?"

Last night, Liv and Alex had skipped a huge annual gala at the Radcliffs', a well-connected family her mother had continuously thrust on her. "Nope. I needed a break from socializing and the press."

"I don't blame you. But really, what do you expect? Your family's fortune—well, yours now…" Rachel reached for Liv's hand and squeezed it for a heartbeat longer than necessary. "Hun, let's face it. Even the Rockefellers would be jealous of you."

"Money doesn't buy happiness." She would trade it all if it would bring her parents back.

"Damn close, though, I bet." Rachel cocked her head.

Toying with the cup of coffee the waiter had delivered, Liv fished for information. "How's work?"

"It's going well." Rachel tucked a piece of honey-blond hair behind her ear. "Are you asking if I got the promotion?"

"Obviously." She grinned back. "I expect to be one of the first you tell. Alex has been very close-lipped regarding when or if you'll get it."

Rachel tapped Liv's hand. "I already heard. That's why I wanted to meet with you. You're looking at the youngest and newest forensic DNA analyst on the New York City Police Department."

Liv jumped to her feet, rushed around the table, and squeezed Rachel in a hug. "I'm so happy for you! But please don't use this as an opportunity to share your experiences on the job." She shuddered. "Some of the work you were doing kept me awake at night."

"Sure it did." Rachel's small body shook with laughter. "With that handsome, hot-blooded, Venezuelan husband of yours filling up your nights?"

Heat suffused Liv's cheeks. Rachel shook her head and stifled her amusement by taking a sip of coffee.

Liv picked at the corner of her napkin, her thoughts darkening. Rarely did they discuss Alex and the police force. As a detective who specialized in drug trafficking, Rachel refused to divulge information that would cause Liv worry. "Is...is there something going on at the office?"

"Always. What do you mean specifically?"

Taking a sip of her drink, Liv debated on how much to say. "It's just that Alex's attitude has been different the past couple of nights. There's this tension rolling off him. Then the other day..."

"What happened?"

"I overheard him on the phone late one night, just a small part of his conversation, really. It was the tone and hour that got to me." Growing up and watching her mother turn a blind eye to her husband's indiscretions hadn't left Liv unscathed. *Alex isn't like that.* Still, that little bit of doubt lodged its way into her mind. She hoped that confiding to Rachel would help dispel her mistrust. "There's something else. He used a different cell phone, because his was on the bedside table."

"Did he say who he was talking to?"

She shook her head, hoping that since Rachel worked with him, she would have some insight. "No. It was the middle of the night. I fell asleep again by the time he came back to bed." A few words had made her think he was referring to their relationship. That had cast doubt over the call being about work.

For the first time since hearing about Alex, Rachel eased back in her chair. "I'm sure it was an informant, especially if he used a different phone and took the call that late. He wouldn't want anyone calling on a cell he'd answer unguarded. It's easier to compartmentalize that way. Hey, don't read into everything he does. He's not your father. I promise I'll tell you if there's anything weird going on that you should hear about. Benefits of working together."

Liv had to let go of her paranoia. "Okay, and I know you would. Thanks."

"The job has been really stressful, and Alex has single-handedly ousted an entire cartel and is on the way to dismantling another one. That's huge. They've halted their control in three states. It's crazy, the intuition he has. If we didn't know any better, I'd swear he had inside experience and firsthand knowledge about the inner workings of drug trafficking and cartels." She shook her head, her eyes taking on a faraway gleam. "So yeah, stress? He probably has it in spades."

"Okay, that's a relief. Well, you get what I mean."

Rachel laughed. "I do."

With that worry cleared up, Liv pressed her lips together, trying to contain the smile playing around the edges. "I have a surprise of my own." Rachel perked up, and Liv blurted out, "I'm pregnant."

"Oh my God, Liv! Have you told Alex?" Rachel rolled her eyes. "Well, of course you have."

Dread pooled in her stomach. "Actually, I haven't." *I need someone to be excited for me.* "He doesn't want kids, Rach."

Rachel's brows furrowed. "Never? Or just so soon after your first year of marriage and your parents…"

Grief stirred in her gut at the mention of her parents who

had died five months ago in a freak accident. "We've never made it past discussing the 'I don't want kids' stage. I'm hoping he'll be happy, that his opinion will change once he gets used to the idea."

"Shit, Liv." Rachel shook her head. "He'll come around. Don't worry."

He'd been so adamant. Liv clasped her hands tight in her lap and plastered on a smile she didn't quite feel. "I'm sure you're right." The twisting in her stomach had nothing to do with morning sickness.

Chapter 2

———

Liv studied Alex as they dined in one of their favorite Italian restaurants. Deep shadows drooped beneath his eyes. Even though he was relaxed, fine lines were etched between his brows. For a few months, she had grieved hard, becoming an emotional zombie after learning of her parents' demise. Her anguish must have taken a toll on him.

While he cut up his chicken in sure strokes, she observed his mannerisms and his features with her artist's eye. His dark hair was disheveled as if he'd run his hands through it a time or two. She saw no slight narrowing of his left eye, which was his telltale sign that something was amiss. Aside from the circles and fine lines, he appeared content. So she relaxed as well—as much as she could with the looming pregnancy discussion.

She swirled a piece of chicken in the sauce before lifting it to her mouth. When she finished chewing, she broke the silence. "How's work going?"

The clatter of his fork against the china caused her eyebrows to rise. In the back of her mind, the phone call he'd had still festered.

He scrubbed his hands over his face. "It's going well. We're very close to bringing in the leader of a drug-trafficking outfit. I'm worried about this one though. This guy is slippery and very dangerous. It's taking more hours, manpower, and skill than I thought it would."

A chill skated across her skin. She dismissed the uncomfortable sensation. Alex's work was a world he mostly kept separate. This was due to his code of ethics, code of conduct, and desire to keep her safe.

The darker elements of his career were not something she cared for. Her only concern was that he was happy and doing what he loved, as she did. How he worked to disassemble drug rings, cartels, and gangs, she would never understand. Nor would she want to be thrust into that dangerous part of his life.

"Is that why you look so exhausted? Or is it because I've been a mess?"

"No, babe. It's not you, never could be. You give me energy. But this job, it's taking a toll. I want out."

She set her fork down and gave him her full attention, wishing she could smooth away the visible stress he wore with a simple touch of her hands. "You told me everything was on track to move into politics with backing from my father, Joe Radcliff, and Davidson, right?" She gnawed on her lip for a second. "I'm assuming my father set up a campaign fund and all the connections you'll need before he passed away?"

Alex's mouth pressed into a grim line. "He did, and I'm damn grateful for it. Although, I'd prefer if your parents were here and the senator position that opened was from your dad retiring instead."

She flinched, reached across the table, and squeezed his hand. "Me too. Even without them here, you've got this, right?"

Relief shone in his face as he grinned. "Yeah, I do. The

governor called me. In a few months, I won't have the worry of my job and all the long hours at the NYPD. It's getting to be too much, and I'm ready for a change. Not much longer now."

Unease danced on the edge of her thoughts, and her smile faltered. "Well, it's a life with its own perils."

Alex shook his head, his eyes shining with excitement. "No, babe. It will be nothing like what you grew up with. We're a team. You're the best thing that's ever happened to me, and I'll never take you for granted."

Warmth filled her with his words. She knew it too. Not a day went by that he didn't do something to make her feel appreciated and loved. The only dark spot that nagged at her was her pregnancy secret, which could shatter their marriage, and the phone call she'd overheard. He'd sworn there were no secrets, and she needed to make peace with it and let it go. Still, her mind clouded over, and her lips pulled down in a frown.

Alex stood, came around the table, and drew her to her feet. "Let it go, Liv," he whispered before placing a heartbreakingly sweet kiss on her forehead.

Aware he didn't realize her thoughts had turned back to the call, she guessed he was talking about his worry over the case and the senate position he hoped to fill. He pulled his chair around the table, settled next to her, and drew her close. In quiet murmurs, they reminisced about everything from when they met and began dating to what they would like to have for lunch tomorrow. She laughed for the first time since her parents' death.

He did that to her—made her happy. She did the same for him. In his embrace, life was simple.

"How's your work going, babe?" Alex asked. "I didn't see any new gallery shows we're scheduled to attend. Everything okay?"

This time, she smiled for real. "We have a small break for the next several months. Giselle is introducing some new artists and wants to properly promote them before the next show.

We'll go to that one." Alex went to the shows for her, not because he enjoyed looking at art. She gave his cheek a slow caress, and her smile dropped away. Fierce emotion kindled, blazed from her heart, and manifested into words. "I love you." Later, she could express her emotion with her body.

Alex paid their bill, and they exited the restaurant, hands interlaced, as they turned to walk back to their apartment. Goose bumps danced along Liv's skin the moment she sensed a change in their environment. Lifting her gaze, she gasped in surprise. The cagey-looking man who'd bumped her earlier headed straight for them. Shaggy brown hair fell in disarray across his forehead, and the jeans and black shirt he wore looked as though they hadn't been washed in a few days. Menace flashed across his face, and her veins felt as if they'd been injected with ice.

Alex tucked her behind him, obstructing her view. Lurching forward, Alex grabbed the man and shoved him against the wall. A dull crack from the man's head crashing against the brick made her cringe.

Liv stood helplessly as heated words volleyed quietly between the two men in Spanish. A few paces behind them, she strained to hear. Over Alex's shoulder, the man sneered at her. She tracked their every move. When the stranger lifted a hand to Alex's arm, her eyes narrowed on the blue ink between his thumb and index finger. She could make out the detail of the sharp-angled butterfly tattoo.

As fast as the altercation happened, it ended. Alex shoved the man away. Whatever he'd said made the stranger hurry down the street. Alex stood motionless, wearing a fierce frown, as he watched him leave.

Alex returned to Liv's side, and despite the miniscule narrowing of his left eye, he flashed a reassuring smile meant to put her at ease. "Informant. Being here, coming anywhere near you was a mistake on his part." He slid his arm around her waist and leaned in to brush a kiss on her cheek. "Ready?"

"If you're sure everything is okay." Her smile wobbled a little, but she firmed it up.

"Yes, of course. Forget about that. This is our night."

"I really don't get how you deal with that."

He tweaked her nose. "Walk in the park, Liv. What's important is you're by my side."

Even with Alex's reassurance that all was well, the man's last words played through her mind as he'd made a hasty departure. His English was heavily accented, and his message was odd. "He's waiting."

Chapter 3

———

STRONG ARMS WRAPPED around her middle, and she leaned into Alex's embrace. She was a chicken. There'd been time to tell him at the restaurant, including the perfect moment when he'd sat beside her and kissed her on the forehead. She'd let it slip away.

Tilting her head back, she smiled. "Morning. Thank you for the flowers. They're beautiful."

He nuzzled her neck. "You're more so."

Desire stirred in her stomach. It would have to wait. Soon, Alex would head out the door for the day. "I wish we had a little more time this morning before your meeting." Reaching a hand back, she threaded her fingers through his thick hair.

"I'm not done, Liv." Turning her in his arms, he brushed his lips across hers, deepening the kiss when she parted for him. He backed her up and pinned her against the counter.

Molded to his body, she let all the tension from the previous night fall away and enjoyed how his mouth moved expertly over hers.

Too soon, he broke their kiss, a grin curving his lips, and he bent to whisper in her ear. "With how quickly everything happened last night, I didn't get a chance to give you a very delayed anniversary gift." His fingers traced the curve of her face, and banked passion blazed in his dark eyes.

A shiver raced down her spine. "Alex, you gave me two cases of my favorite wine from Savage Seas Winery for our one year. I told you that was the only thing I wanted." Their first anniversary had been six months ago, one month before the accident.

"It wasn't enough. Never is with you. I want to shower you in gifts." His shoulders tensed for the merest second. "You understand why we couldn't go on our honeymoon right away?"

Her smile softened, and she played with the ends of his hair at the back of his head. "Of course. Please stop worrying about that. There will be time for us to travel together. I get how important your work is to you. The timing wasn't right."

He grimaced. "I was so close to busting open the entire south-side cartel and mafia connection. It paid off, us waiting."

"It did. You're brilliant, and shutting the drug-trafficking factions down advanced your career by years. I couldn't be more proud of you. Just think how that'll impact the children who are exposed to that. You're saving lives for future genera-tions. Even ours."

"Babe, we've talked about this. We can't have kids. I don't want them used against me. And they would be. It's just not a good idea." He softened his words by pressing a kiss to her pouting lips.

She frowned, her stomach a caldron of anxiety about telling him. Now was definitely not the time.

His grimace shifted to a grin. "At least with all the hours I put in, you had time to sculpt. You've grown. The finished pieces you sold at the gallery prove that. Although, I have my eye on the dancer you just glazed. Think we may have to keep that."

"You saw her? It's not in any shape for you to see yet. I need to fire it." She nibbled her lip, holding back her laughter, and very grateful for the change of subject. "Thanks for believing in me." Her parents had not when it came to sculpting, and the mantle of responsibility she'd worn weighed on her soul. When she had married Alex, he took a large portion of the burden off her.

"Be proud of what you are." He must have noticed where her train of thought had gone. "You're an artist, Liv. Your parents' goals don't define you." Before he could blink them away, dark shadows swirled in his eyes.

For the hundredth time, she wondered what secrets lived in his past. Someday he would confide in her. Refusing to let her insecurities be an influence, she rose up on her toes and kissed his cheek.

"Liv, I want to give you something before I leave for work." He drew a velvet box from his pocket and opened it. "It was my grandmother's."

Her hand fluttered to her mouth, and her gaze found his. An intricate silver design held a round stone of mercurial blues and purples. The antique setting looked very old.

Intense love collided with the swirling darkness that danced through his eyes. She recognized the strong emotion and the vulnerability that flashed in his brown depths on rare occasions. This piece of him, of his past with a grandmother he'd adored, meant a great deal, and the emotional weight of it caused her hands to shake. If only she'd had a chance to meet the woman before she'd died, or his mother, for that matter, who lived in Venezuela. For reasons Liv didn't fully understand, his mother had missed their wedding. "It's beautiful. I'm honored, Alex."

"I would have given it to you sooner, but after last night, I thought this was the perfect time to give you my grandmother's brooch."

Her brow furrowed. *After the confrontation when we left the restaurant?*

"My mother said this was my grandmother's favorite piece, one she kept with her always. Now, as my wife, it belongs to you"—he grinned—"even though I know you don't wear pins."

Laughter filled the air, and they said in unison, "Because they ruin clothes."

He tweaked her nose. "Our jeweler has the measurements and picture. This is temporary—the charm bracelet it's on. I think having it dangle like that could cause it to be hit too often and break. I'm going to have it mounted onto another design, one with a thin silver cuff."

"It's lovely, Alex." She ran her fingers over the smooth, fiery blue-green stone. *Paraiba tourmaline, perhaps?* A beat passed, and the air thickened as she looked from the gift to him. The strange seriousness of his expression caused her to pay closer attention to his next words.

"You hold both my past and future in your hands."

———

Continue reading Broken Circle, book one in the Gray Ghost series.

https://amymckinleyauthor.com/gray-ghost-series/

———

Keep up with Amy's releases by joining her newsletter!
http://eepurl.com/ghzRjD

ABOUT THE AUTHOR

 Amy McKinley is the *USA Today* Bestselling author of the romantic suspense thriller Gray Ghost Novels, Deadly Isles Special Ops, Covert Recruits, Moonlit Destination Series, the Five Fates paranormal romance books, and several standalone titles. Her edge-of-your-seat books are filled with surprising twists and just the right amount of heat and danger. She lives in Illinois with her husband, two daughters, two sons, and three mischievous cats.

ALSO BY AMY MCKINLEY

Gray Ghost Novels

Moments That Define Us

Broken Circle

Eye of the Storm

Beneath the Surface

Vantage Point

Covert Threat

Marked for Death

Deadly Isles Special Ops

Hidden Secrets

Twisted Secrets

Bound by Secrets

Forged by Secrets

Covert Recruits (coming soon)

Irina

Sasha

Zena

Nadia

Katya

Standalone Titles

Shattered Melody

Siren's Call: Cursed Seas

Fake Fiancé (A Second Chance Office Romance)

Moonlit Destination Series

Moonlit Whisper

Moonlit Kiss

Moonlit Mirage

Five Fates Series

Hidden

Taken

www.ingramcontent.com/pod-product-compliance
Lightning Source LLC
Chambersburg PA
CBHW070955190726
48292CB00004B/1470